She dream... ...b...
Marco and ...

They were play... ...
beach. Marco ...
towards Ben, an...
he'd missed it ...
upset and started calling for her, sobbing,
'I want my mummy,' and then he changed it to,
'I want my daddy'. The words rang out over and
over again, then Marco was scooping Ben into his
arms and Ben stopped crying, hugging him,
laughing...

'Do you want to say "Hello, Daddy" in Italian?'

'Yes.'

'*Ciao, Papà.*'

'*Chow, Pappa.*'

'*Si, va bene. Ciao, Papà. Molto bene!*'

'*Molto benny?* What's that?'

'Very good. Your Italian is very good.'

Polly opened her eyes. The voices in her dream
were real. The conversation was taking place right
here in her bedroom.

'Mummy's awake!' Ben pointed out, pleased. He
jumped out of bed and climbed onto hers, bouncing
up and down excitedly, 'Mummy, Daddy's here.
He's going to stay with us always now...'

Having abandoned her first intended career for marriage, **Rosalie Ash** spent several years as a bilingual personal assistant to the managing director of a leisure group. She now lives in Warwickshire, with her husband, and daughters Kate and Abby, and her lifelong enjoyment of writing has led to her career as a novelist. Her interests include languages, travel and research for her books, reading, and visits to the Royal Shakespeare Theatre in nearby Stratford-upon-Avon. Other pleasures include swimming, yoga and country walks.

Recent titles by the same author:

A FRAGILE MARRIAGE

THE IDEAL FATHER

BY
ROSALIE ASH

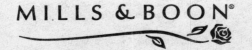

MILLS & BOON®

First published in Great Britain 1998
Harlequin Mills & Boon Limited,
Eton House, 18-24 Paradise Road, Richmond, Surrey TW9 1SR

© Rosalie Ash 1998

ISBN 0 263 81143 3

Set in Times Roman 9½ on 10½ pt.
01-9809-63018 C1

Printed and bound in Norway
by AiT Trondheim AS, Trondheim

CHAPTER ONE

THE family christening party, on a sunny hillside in Tuscany, was crowded with people generating a happy atmosphere. Polly felt foolish for ever doubting the warmth of her own welcome.

The two wicker cots stood in the shade of a gnarled wisteria against the wall of the solid stone Tuscan farmhouse. Pushing her hair from her face, Polly peered in cautiously. The two tiny dark-haired babies lay side by side. Twins. Marco's new little nieces. They were both in snowy christening robes, both on their backs, with their diminutive left thumbs jammed in their mouths.

As she watched, the tiny mouths sucked spasmodically, the eyelids flickered, screwed up, then relaxed. Small fingers flexed and sleepily fell still again. Safe in their own little worlds. Dreaming whatever three-week-old babies dreamed about, Polly thought, smiling softly. The babies' features, their colouring and skin-tone, had a familiar look about them; they made her think of Ben when he was a baby. Her insides tightened. She admitted to herself, with a silent jolt, precisely why she was really here.

She couldn't pretend that she'd merely bowed to Dad's pressure to come to Italy. True, Dad *had* exerted an unexpected amount of pressure on her to accept the Darettas' invitation to this christening party—mainly, she suspected, to show that the English Hamiltons and the Sicilian Darettas, two sides of the same family, had finally stopped feuding. And since the only Daretta she had a problem with was Marco, and her stepsister Sophy had told her he'd be tied up on a court case in London, she'd agreed to come.

But who was she fooling? Leaving aside any noble intentions, her reasons for being here were emotional, very personal, and not in the least bit rational. Marco Daretta was uncle to twin baby girls. Succumbing to her father's pleas for family unity had merely been her excuse to give in to the temptation to see them,

5

to see some fresh examples of Daretta family offspring, torture herself, secretly compare notes...

She stared tenderly at the sleeping babies. Marco's sister, Marietta, was half-English, like Marco, but her husband was Italian, of course. And yet there it was, the unmistakable Daretta family likeness, Polly decided, even in the tiny, unformed features. The Daretta genes, no doubt extra potent with centuries of dark Sicilian blood, were powerfully dominant, whoever they happened to mate with.

She leaned a little closer. Had these babies inherited the stunning blue-black Daretta eyes? Impossible to tell at the moment. They were both fast asleep. Their lashes, luxuriously thick against the peachy curve of their cheeks, were sooty black.

'Polly.'

At the unexpected sound of Marco's husky voice she jumped violently, guiltily, as if she'd been caught doing something she shouldn't. Immediately she felt angry with herself. She was working very hard at not feeling guilty any more.

She jerkily straightened up and turned round, blonde hair swinging back from her face. It took a huge amount of self-control to keep a polite, composed expression on her face as she looked up at the man beside her. But speech seemed temporarily impossible. She just stared at him, her heart thudding in panic.

'Aren't you going to say hello?' he prompted helpfully. Marco's dark forehead was creased with a frown. The black-fringed eyes were politely enquiring.

He had extraordinary eyes. Deep-set, beneath thick black brows. His irises were a brilliant shade of dark blue that had always made her think of blue-black permanent ink, the kind her father still kept on his bureau in old-fashioned glass bottles.

She ran her tongue nervously over her lips, cleared her throat. 'Hello, Marco.'

'We finally get to meet again. How are you, Polly?' He was assessing her from head to foot. 'Are you well?'

She knew she must be managing to smile. With a kind of panicky self-awareness she could feel her lips moving into the appropriate curve.

If only she'd been prepared for this. She'd rehearsed meeting

Marco again many times over the last four years. She'd been due to meet him on a couple of occasions, but had lost courage each time and made an excuse to cancel at the last minute. She hadn't really known how she'd react at the sight of him.

Now, she registered dimly that she was shaking. Her solar plexus churned in sick panic. The warm breeze was ruffling her hair, and her soft brick-coloured linen suit was probably creased from travelling. She felt his eyes move briefly down over her figure, taking in the slim skirt which finished demurely just above the knee, the taupe suede court shoes lifting her normal five feet four inches by three inches. When he raised his eyes to skim the discreet suggestion of cleavage at the vee of her short-sleeved jacket, she felt her body betray her with a twist of reaction in her stomach, a tightening around her nipples.

She despised herself for this. She always felt inadequate under Marco's close scrutiny, always felt that Marco must be comparing her with Sophy, and, if he thought about her at all, be noting what a pale, inferior shadow she made to her stepsister's sultry glamour.

She and Sophy did share similar colouring—pure coincidence, since they were not blood relatives—and a description of both of them on paper would sound remarkably alike: fair, Anglo-Saxon, blue eyes, long blonde hair. Even their physical characteristics could sound identical: short, slightly tilted nose, full mouth, slender build. But in the flesh the similarities vanished.

Sophy had that elusive 'something' which drove men crazy. Her figure was curvier, she was so much taller, her colouring more dramatic, her sexual self-assurance legendary. Polly only had to think about her stepsister to see the image of her in Marco's arms, of the two of them locked in a hungry embrace, the way she'd seen them five years ago in Sicily, and the way she imagined, from Sophy's regular reminders, the two of them spent most of their time together to this day...

Polly breathed in slowly, willing herself to be calm. Peace and serenity were just a deep breath away; that was what her anti-stress self-hypnosis tapes and her yoga teacher assured her.

'I'm fine, thanks. And you look well, Marco,' she managed at last.

He looked more than well; he looked...gorgeous, she decided ruefully, eyeing his masculine perfection. His slate-coloured suit was a triumph of Italian tailoring, his blue-grey shirt and soft terracotta and blue striped tie were subtly elegant. Just looking at him, at the hard-boned angles of his face, his eyes, the warm olive skin, the glossy black slightly unruly hair, increased the sick, tight feeling inside her.

'I wasn't expecting you to be here today,' she said, when the silence became protracted.

'Really? But this is my house. Why would I host my sister's christening party and not attend in person?'

This remote farmhouse, isolated in undulating acres of cornfields and vines and olive groves and red Tuscan earth, was Marco's? Polly frowned faintly, cross with herself for not knowing. The invitation had come from Marietta, and it had been his mother, Aunt Ruth, she'd spoken to on the telephone when she'd accepted.

But now that she thought about it, of course he'd be closely involved in the christening of his sister's babies. His court appearances in London wouldn't keep him away. If ever there was a committed family man, it was Marco Daretta, she thought bleakly. After all, he was half-Sicilian. Her aunt Ruth had told her that the only institution in the Sicilian conscience that really counted was the family. For Marco, no doubt family came first. Babies in particular would come high on his list of priorities. It just depended which side of the family was involved.

And whose baby...

Polly suppressed a small shudder of apprehension. The enormity of her decision, taken after months of agonising uncertainty four years ago, had abruptly manifested itself like a lead weight in her heart...

'Polly, darling! You made it!' Aunt Ruth's delighted exclamation defused the mounting tension. Polly swung away from Marco, allowing herself to be hugged by Marco's mother, soft and pretty in a toffee silk dress, then scrutinised by warm hazel eyes, the affection she read there making her relax a little. 'My dear, I'm so glad you could come!'

'Me too,' she said huskily. 'Sorry Dad and Sophy couldn't make it.'

'Don't worry, I quite understand.'

'Dad was in the middle of a court case,' Polly went on quickly, 'and Sophy had a modelling assignment.'

'Having you here makes up for it. You're my stepbrother's child, Polly. And how many times have we met over the years?'

'Well...' Polly smiled slightly. 'Once or twice?'

'Twice. Once in England—when you were only about thirteen? And that Easter holiday, when you came on that trip to Sicily with us just before you started university,' Ruth reminded her with a rueful laugh. 'I was hoping Marietta's babies would give everyone the excuse for a nice big family reunion. I can't deny I'd have loved to see my brother here today...'

'I know...' Polly bit her lip. 'How long is it since you saw each other?'

Ruth made a rueful face.

'It must be...oh, about ten years since I saw Harry, and that wasn't exactly a happy meeting. I'd come to see my mother, let Marco meet his English grandmother. She practically threw us both out...'

'Dad wanted to come, Aunt Ruth,' Polly said loyally, her eyes steady as she met her aunt's. 'Truly...'

This *was* the truth, Polly reflected; her father was a proud man, who found it difficult to make the first move in patching up quarrels. Whilst he was too proud to actually renew proper contact himself, he'd long since stopped feeling any animosity towards the Darettas. He'd made no objection to Polly and Sophy's holiday with them in Sicily, five years earlier, and this invitation to the christening would have given him the perfect, face-saving opportunity for a reunion with his sister Ruth—and the Sicilian chef she'd flouted Hamilton approval by marrying twenty-nine years ago.

'He was very disappointed,' Polly went on. 'So was Sophy. She'd have been here like a shot, if she could. They send their love—and pressies, of course!' She held up the Harrods carrier-bag with a lop-sided grin. 'The babies are adorable!'

'Darling, I know! They're little miracles. Do you want to hold one?'

'Take care, Mother,' Marco said. He sounded drily amused. 'Marietta says if you wake the babies to show them off once more she'll put you on night duty for a week.'

Ruth looked sheepish.

'Oh, dear, have they fallen asleep again? I've never known such sleepy babies. If they can sleep through this racket, they'll sleep through anything. Marco, darling, isn't it lovely to have Polly here?'

There was a pause.

'Lovely,' he said gravely. 'She's a very evasive lady.' Then Polly felt the blood rush to her face and neck as Marco closed firm fingers over her shoulders and kissed her formally on each cheek.

Polly went still. She felt the heat of his fingers on her skin, the brush of stubble against her cheek, smelled a trace of some subtle citrus sandalwood cologne which was warm and clean and male, and uniquely Marco...

She felt annoyed at how powerfully he could affect her. But he'd always had this effect on her. Hardly hearing the conversation continuing around her, she found herself thinking about when she'd first met Marco ten years ago. She'd been thirteen; he'd have been twenty-one. Tall, loose-limbed, athletic, he'd come storming out of Hamilton Priory after the confrontation with his grandmother that Ruth had just mentioned.

She'd been coming home from school. Seeing him on the steps of her grandmother Hamilton's house, she'd stopped abruptly and nearly got flattened by the paperboy, whizzing out of the bushes at the end of the long drive, going much too fast on his mountain bike. Marco had seen the accident about to happen, leaped forward and pulled her out of the way just in time. Her school bag had gone flying, scattering books over the gravel, and the paperboy had crashed off his bike. He'd clambered up quickly, redfaced, muttering apologies. Marco had kept hold of Polly's shoulders, to steady her against falling. He'd said, 'Are you all right?' in a distracted, husky voice, and he must have said something else, too, only she hadn't been listening, because her impressionable, thirteen-year-old imagination had been caught up in the extraordinary power of that slanting dark blue gaze, the untidy black hair and large, dark, brooding features.

What a pity Grandma Hamilton wasn't still alive and here today, Polly thought fleetingly now. Because she'd have been able to see that her stepdaughter Ruth's 'disgraceful' behaviour with her penniless Sicilian chef had led to a devoted, loving marriage and a large, close-knit family; she'd have been able to see that the first fruit of that union, her step-grandson Marco, was a successful barrister. Surely that was what really mattered to every parent, wasn't it? Knowing that their children, and their children's children, were successful, happy and loved?

Polly's thoughts stopped abruptly at this point. Happy 'ideal families' were hardly her strong point, were they?

She'd gone hot again—a heat unrelated to the warmth of an Italian summer.

'I caught Polly clucking over the babies,' Marco was saying, with a grin. 'I hadn't realised she was the maternal type.'

She found herself holding her breath. The hot feeling intensified, then turned to cold as a wave of panic swept over her. She felt sick, almost faint with fright. Did he *know*? She jerked her head quickly to see the expression in his eyes, but the ink-blue gaze was bland. No, he couldn't possibly know, Polly told herself shakily. If he did, he wouldn't be making polite, jokey conversation with her; he'd be coldly, furiously angry, just as, maybe, he'd have a right to be...

'How come you're qualified to pass judgement on what "type" I am, Marco?' she said, willing her voice not to tremble. 'We haven't seen each other for years.'

'Your fault, Polly, not mine. I'm probably basing my opinion on out-of-date information, but you were partying quite strenuously last time we met.'

'A lot can change in four years.'

'You know, I believe you *have* changed, Polly.' His eyes flicked over her again, examining everything: the long silky hair, a shade of pale barley, tumbling around her shoulders, the wide grey-blue eyes. 'You look...more mature. More serene. It suits you.'

'Really?' It was all she could find to say; her throat felt painfully dry.

She'd done the right thing, she told herself, in silent desperation. She'd done the only thing possible. To have told Marco about her pregnancy, when he'd made it clear he'd be appalled at such a complication, would have been too humiliating. And to have told him afterwards, when Ben was born...impossible. She caught her breath involuntarily as the agony of those past decisions came back to her.

Ben had been conceived during one reckless, thoughtless moment of desire—at least on Marco's part. And even if Marco *had* wanted more, she'd have been morally bound to say no and stay right out of his range. Marco was Sophy's property.

Sophy made that clear every time she came home to Hamilton Priory. If she registered the tell-tale likeness of Ben to Marco, she gave no sign. And she never stopped telling Polly how often Marco had rung her from abroad, or spent the night at her flat in London, or how often they'd gone away together for a weekend, or how he'd bought her sexy lingerie or expensive jewellery for her birthday...

She'd have been doing the unthinkable—embarking on an affair with her stepsister's lover...

But that complication hadn't arisen. Marco had made it clear that night that he didn't want to get involved with her, that their lovemaking had been impulsive, a one-off mistake best forgotten...

But suddenly none of these logical justifications helped. She still felt paralysed by the knowledge that right now, in England, there was a small boy being cared for by family friends while she was here in Italy, and that he was Marco's son—no, *their* son, her's and Marco's—and that Marco had no idea...

'Marco, stop teasing and get Polly some wine, darling,' Ruth ordered her son chidingly. 'Look after her. She's come all the way from England. Make her feel at home.'

'Don't make me sound like a martyr, Aunt Ruth,' Polly said with a slight laugh. 'It didn't seem far to travel for the pleasure of seeing Marietta's twins!'

One of the babies stirred and gave a little squeak, and on cue the other one woke up. They both started to cry. Marietta appeared out of nowhere in a cobalt-blue dress which revealed a more rounded figure than Polly remembered, but she was still as glowingly beautiful as ever, the reddish lights in her long dark hair the only trace of the English blood inherited from Ruth.

All the Daretta offspring were stunning, Polly reflected, from Marco right down to his last sister, and they all bore the Daretta hallmarks of dark, dramatic Sicilian good looks. She reflected again how powerfully the blood of dark Sicilian dominated delicate English Rose. All trace of Hamilton features had been wiped out, as if in apt revenge for the years of disapproval.

'Mamma, did you prod them again?'

'On my honour, Marietta, I was nowhere near them,' Ruth protested, eyes wide. 'Tell her, Marco, Polly, was it me?'

They were all laughing as Marietta promptly handed one baby to Marco and one to Polly, giving Polly a welcoming kiss as she did so.

'You were nearest when they woke, so you can look after them for a while!' she said, as she sat down and unwrapped the presents from the Harrods bag, exclaiming in delight over the pair of hallmarked solid silver photograph frames and sets of porcelain Peter Rabbit plates, dishes and mugs.

'They're from all of us—Dad and Sophy as well.'

'They're gorgeous! Thank you so much...' Marietta had started laughing at Marco's bemused expression as he inspected the squirming infant in his arms. 'Time you got some practise in, brother dear, for when you answer Papà's prayers and give him a grandson!'

Ruth eyed her daughter with mock reproof.

'Marietta, you know your father is in seventh heaven to have twin granddaughters! Besides, I'd prefer it if Marco found a wife first!'

'Shouldn't be too difficult,' his sister observed, 'he's had enough of Europe's eligible females hanging on his arm during the last few years.'

'A gross exaggeration,' Marco drawled, deadpan. 'And even if it were true, what's wrong with playing the field?'

'Of course, poor Marco. Life's too short to rush into commitment to the wrong woman, isn't it?' Marietta teased.

Polly winced inwardly. She'd had direct experience of this no strings, no commitment philosophy from Marco. She'd seen at first hand how he reacted when faced with even the remotest possibility of being trapped as a consequence of his own actions. How did Sophy stand it? she wondered. But maybe Sophy preferred her freedom too. She moved in glamorous modelling circles, travelled a lot; it probably suited her to meet up with Marco as and when their diaries coincided...

Marco jiggled the howling baby in his arms, but his efforts to quell the crying were unsuccessful. Polly found his perplexed, frowning expression somehow perversely amusing.

Cradling the other baby against her shoulder, she patted her gently on the back, surprising her into silence. A pair of dark blue, black-fringed eyes regarded her with the guileless, unblinking curiosity of the very young. She caught Marco's eye, and couldn't contain her mirth any longer.

'Precisely how did you do that?' Marco demanded. He was inspecting his own charge, whose small red face was growing more and more contorted with rage, not a tear to be seen.

'Maybe she's the extrovert of the two?' She was struggling with her giggles. The glimmer of rueful amusement in Marco's dark face was doing devastating things to her self-control. 'Or maybe she's just hungrier?'

Taking pity on him, Marietta retrieved her small daughter and went in search of feeding bottles. On impulse, Polly carefully placed her own gurgling bundle into Marco's arms. The baby gazed up at Marco in wide-eyed curiosity, and then smiled at him, patting his face in apparent delight.

'At least one of my nieces seems to approve of me,' Marco pointed out, with an air of relief. 'I was starting to think I'd lost my touch.'

'Your touch?'

'Babies like me, in general.' He grinned, relinquishing the child to his mother as she held out her arms for her grandchild. His dignity and self-esteem were restored, Polly reflected, wryly relieved as well. Then she despised herself for caring about

Marco's self-esteem one way or another. He hadn't cared much about hers at their last encounter...

'Go and get something to eat and drink, Polly darling.' Ruth smiled, cuddling the baby. 'Marco will look after you.'

'Would I dare to disobey?' he teased gently, ushering Polly away as instructed.

He steered her towards the long, white-clothed table beneath the shade of the wisteria. Obviously the family and guests had all sat down together to eat, and Polly had arrived too late to join them. A cluster of elderly black-clad relatives lingered at one end of the table, talking and drinking, watching the celebrations with smiling eyes through a haze of cigarette smoke.

With slightly constrained formality, Marco pulled out a chair for her at the other end.

'The babies really are gorgeous, aren't they?' she said, trying to think of something to say to ease the tension.

'Naturally. They are Daretta babies,' Marco said. 'And they are my goddaughters.'

She widened her eyes mockingly. 'So you're a *godfather* as well as an uncle now?'

The expression in Marco's eyes dropped several degrees in temperature. Polly instantly regretted the teasing tone of her remark. Maybe Marco's Sicilian ancestry had made him touchy about the alternative connotations of the title and role of godfather. She'd heard Grandma Hamilton make enough acid comments to her father over the years to realise that the Darettas could be sensitive about that...

'Yes. It's a great honour. I plan to take my responsibilities very seriously. I'm sorry you were too late to join us for the meal,' he said stiffly.

'My flight was delayed,' she explained. She sat very still as he deftly gathered up pasta, salad, bread, cheese and wine, and arrayed them around her. 'And, then there was a mix-up over the hired car. I messed around at the airport so long trying to sort it all out, I thought I'd never get here.'

And now she wished with all her heart that he would just go away and leave her to eat alone. Aunt Ruth meant well, but if she only knew Marco was the last person on earth Polly would choose to 'look after' her.

'It's a miracle that you came at all,' he said drily. 'I was starting to think that the Fates would keep us apart until our next incarnation. So welcome to my house, Polly. Here, have some Chianti.' He poured the red wine into her glass, then poured some for himself. His gaze glinted beneath heavy lids as he settled into a chair opposite, watching her intently. 'Do you like my Tuscan home?'

She felt herself reddening slightly, wishing for the thousandth time that her fair skin didn't show quite so obviously when she was embarrassed. His wry sarcasm was probably justified, in part. She *had* managed to quite deftly avoid him over the last four years. But his reasons for arranging to meet her couldn't possibly have had more justification than her reasons for dodging him...

Taking a deep breath, she took hold of her shaky poise, glanced behind her at the ancient stone walls and rust-red shutters, then around her at the extraordinary beauty of the landscape, the bright flowers, the delphinium sky, the deep red earth.

'That goes without saying,' she said frankly. 'I love this place. How much time do you get to spend here?'

'Not enough,' he admitted, stretching his arms behind his head and gazing around him. The physical movement made his suit jacket fall open. Polly found herself fighting against the urge to stare at the expanse of hard male chest beneath the soft fabric of his shirt. 'I spend too much time in cities.'

'I don't know how you can bear to leave it.'

'It will always be here when I get back. It has a timeless feel, don't you think? There is a special quality of light, here in Tuscany.'

'And a special smell,' she agreed. 'Herbs and flowers and warm earth...'

She followed his gaze down the hillside. The terrace ran the full length of the house, dotted with stone statues and urns. Beyond the terrace, some rather crumbling stone steps led down to a grassy slope, and beyond that undulating hills stretched as far as she could see, smothered with ripening shoots of corn and fresh vine leaves and olives, in shades of green and gold and russet, all the way down to Florence.

'It's like a Giorgione painting,' she murmured, 'that golden glow over everything. It's hard to believe real people actually live here.'

'You drove up from the airport. You must have seen some "real people", Polly?'

She had a brief mental recall of small dusty villages, washing flapping, small children playing in the dust and old men in black watching her pass from the shade of their local bars.

'You're right. I did.' She blinked in the dark intensity of his gaze, and cast about for something else to say to keep polite, wary conversation going. 'It was kind of you to host the christening party here, Marco. Where does Marietta live?'

'Marietta and her husband have a small flat in Florence. My parents are in the middle of re-roofing their villa, further down the hill. My house seemed the ideal place.'

'How long have you owned it?'

'About six months.' He glanced around with narrowed eyes. 'I've got plans to renovate a bit; there's an ancient swimming pool down there beyond the terrace, which is useable but could do with rebuilding—I know a stonemason who'll do a good job—and there's maintenance work to be done which I just haven't had time to organise. The terrace needs renovation, for a start—the parapet and steps are crumbling.'

'If you've only owned it for six months, you can hardly expect to have everything done already. I imagine you're pretty tied up with your work?'

He nodded wryly. 'In London, I always dreamed of owning my own place in Italy. I can unwind here...' He paused, his eyes focussing suddenly on hers, making her feel pinned to the spot. 'Tell me how you're getting on in England,' he said at last, smiling slightly. 'Is your father well?'

'He's fine. He works too hard, I think...' Her father had been widowed twice. As far as Polly understood what went on behind her father's usual reserve, he seemed to live for his work.

'Judges don't retire early, as a rule,' Marco commented, without inflection.

'Do...do you meet up with him at all? Professionally, I mean...?'

'I don't come across him very often—a lot of my work is outside the UK these days. But whenever I see him in court he seems in good health. He's reputed to be a good judge, quite wise and fair.' Marco's tone was dry. Polly winced slightly. No doubt 'wise and fair' were not words to loom large in Marco's impression of the older generation of Hamiltons. 'And what are you doing these days?' Marco added.

'I'm back home in Hamilton Priory now. I...run my own business from there...'

'Really? I had no idea. Sophy said nothing about it.'

'You and Sophy *are* still seeing each other, then?' As soon as she'd blurted this she could have bitten out her tongue. Had she begun to entertain some vague, romantic fantasy that Sophy could have been exaggerating her closeness to Marco? She despised herself for being so gullible.

She knew perfectly well that Marco and Sophy were still involved with each other. Whenever she saw her stepsister, Marco's name was rarely absent from the conversation. But she hadn't seen Sophy very often recently. It was a mutual arrangement. Sophy, two years older, was the daughter of Harry Hamilton's second wife. Polly's mother had died adventurously climbing a mountain in India, when Polly was ten. Sadly, Sophy's mother had died during a late-in-life pregnancy, and, despite Polly's hopeful efforts to acquire a friendly 'older sister', the two girls had ended up at best tolerating and at worst detesting each other.

'Seeing each other?' Marco looked as if he were mulling over the precise definition of the phrase, like a barrister might in cross-examination of a witness. 'We speak on the telephone, and we often get together if we're both in London. In fact, she came out here a couple of months ago, to see the new house. Why? Do you disapprove?'

Polly was aware of an all too familiar unpleasant cold sensation taking hold just beneath her breastbone, banishing her appetite completely. It was a totally irrational, jealous despair, and she hated herself for still feeling it, even when she'd had five years to get used to the fact that Marco was seeing Sophy... The pasta suddenly tasted like sawdust.

'Disapprove?' Her echo held the necessary note of incredulity. 'Why on earth should I disapprove?'

He shrugged, drinking some wine. His watchful gaze made her shift uneasily in her chair.

A vivid image of Marco and Sophy, dining together in some fashionable London bistro before going back to make love all night in Sophy's flat, rose unbidden. She felt sick. What was the matter with her? She'd lived with this knowledge for years. She'd based all her actions, her vital decisions for her future, around this knowledge.

She'd never banished the guilt and shame she'd felt after that weekend of the Ball in Cambridge, knowing that Marco was involved with Sophy...

'You look tense, Polly.' Marco's abrupt comment stopped this train of thought in its tracks. 'My mother told me you were only planning on staying one night. Can't you stay longer? Take the chance to relax?'

'No.'

Relax? With Marco around? She could hardly believe he could be so thick-skinned. But he probably had no idea of how much he'd hurt her four years ago, she reminded herself fairly. He'd have no idea of the havoc he'd caused in her life. And she couldn't, didn't dare allow him to find out.

'I can't afford any more time away,' she added, to sweeten the refusal slightly.

Marco passed her the bread, taking a chunk for himself, which he began to eat thoughtfully with some of the black olives and cheese. He sipped his wine.

'From your business?'

'Yes. I've started my own genealogical agency. Tracing people's family trees...'

'Yes, I do know what genealogy is.'

She saw his wry smile, and pulled a face.

'Sorry. Yes, I'm sure you do.'

'So...you enjoy it? Is the business going well?'

'Yes, to the first question. I love it. And to the second...' She hesitated slightly, anxious not to convey her precarious situation to him. 'It depends on how you define "going well". It's never going to make me rich. But it's early days yet. And my overheads are quite low as I work from home. I had one of the stable blocks converted into an office...'

Discussing the details of her home and working life with Marco made her nervous. She couldn't be sure where his line of questioning was leading. She gabbled quickly on, 'Dad was quite enthusiastic—genealogy has been his passion for years. That's how he came to buy Hamilton Priory. Did you know that? He traced the Hamilton family tree back to the thirteenth century, and then bought back the ancestral family home!'

'I expect that pleased the grandparents,' said Marco. 'Confirmation of their well-connected origins.'

'Careful.' She kept her voice light. 'You've never struck me as the type to have a serious chip on your shoulder, Marco.'

His wide mouth thinned.

'Haven't I?' His grin was suddenly ruthless. 'Well, if I've survived without one, it's no thanks to the Hamilton side of the family, is it, Polly?'

She felt herself grow hot with defensive loyalty to her family.

'Don't resurrect the past, Marco. Rifts never get healed if people keep tearing them open again...'

'True,' he said flatly, his mouth twisting. 'And we're rambling from the point. It must be the hot Italian sun and this excellent Chianti.'

'What point have we rambled from?' She frowned, meeting Marco's shuttered gaze.

'I was trying to persuade you to take a short holiday from your business. What's to stop you from spending a little longer in Tuscany? Surely the pressures of genealogical research can't be so great?'

She found herself staring at him, her heart thumping.

'I don't like to be away from home too long.'

'You're only twenty-three.' He spoke reflectively. 'Surely young enough to stay a few nights away from home, to enjoy some fun in your life?'

'Last time we met, I seem to recall you advising me to seek a little *less* fun in my life, Marco.'

She'd made the sharp retort without thinking. She felt her colour begin to rise.

'As the last time we met was at that Ball in Cambridge, Polly, perhaps it's a question of balance,' he suggested. There was a marked coolness in his voice now. She winced.

She turned her head to face him, and found her eyes locked with a relentless blue-black gaze.

She caught her lip in her teeth, willing her cheeks to cool. The intensity of the sudden flood of memories left her feeling weak at the knees. She smiled at him cautiously, picked up her wine-glass with a shaky hand, and sipped with careful precision.

'Can we talk about something else?' she enquired, with delicate insistence. 'I'm afraid my ego takes rather a battering whenever I think about that.'

Marco stood up slowly and came around the table. He pulled up a chair beside her. He leant one arm casually along the back of her chair. She could feel the heat of his body, even through his suit. His nearness sent her into a state of near panic. She held her breath until the ridiculous pumping of her heart had slowed.

'It shouldn't,' Marco reasoned huskily. 'What happened wasn't your fault; it was mine. If I'd exercised self-control it would never have happened. In fact...' He drew a deep breath and visibly took control of his brooding air of anger. 'I'm glad you've raised the subject, Polly. Since you walked out that day without even saying goodbye, we've never had the chance to clear the air.'

She bit her lip, and drank some more wine. Marco's closeness was playing havoc with her blood pressure, his unexpected intensity probing dangerously beneath her defences. 'We're resurrecting the past again, Marco. Let's leave it where it belongs. Forgotten.'

'Unfortunately,' he said quietly, 'that kind of thing is hard to forget.'

Polly stared at him. Her throat felt tight with choked emotion.

'If you expect me to believe that you've given it a single thought all this time, you really do take me for a fool!'

'Why do you say that?'

There was a cool pause. Pride kept her silent.

'*I'm* not a fool, Polly.' Marco's voice was harsh when he continued. 'You've been avoiding me on every occasion where we might have met up and talked about what happened. Believe it or not, the feel of my nineteen-year-old step-cousin clutching me in her arms, begging me to make love to her, has lingered in my memory for a surprisingly long time.'

Polly stood up. Her knees were feeling annoyingly boneless.

'You're enjoying this, aren't you?' she protested quietly. 'Excuse me, I think I'll go and offer my services to Marietta...'

Marco stood up too. She had the uncomfortable sensation of being towered over.

'I'm sorry, Polly. I can see you still find the thought of what happened...distasteful. But you're the one who brought this subject up.' The darkening in his eyes made her think of the ocean before a storm. 'You can hardly blame me if the occasion now comes back to me in graphic detail.'

His words hung in the air between them, like invisible missiles. Find the thought of what happened *distasteful*? What was he talking about? It had been one of the definitively wonderful moments of her life; it was scorched indelibly on her memory.

She suddenly had an absurd desire to turn and run to her car and drive back to the airport at hectic speed. She could put up with Marco disapproving of her, with Marco mocking her. But Marco looking at her as if...as if he actually cared about what had happened... It felt like the last straw. The sudden tug of remembered desire was dark and hot in her stomach.

He was scanning her flushed face, his gaze lidded.

'Stay over tomorrow night, Polly,' he suggested quietly. 'I'd like time to show you some of Tuscany.'

Polly couldn't tear her eyes from his face.

'*Per favore?*' The husky use of Italian was designed to coax and charm, she knew. She clenched her nails into the palms of her fists, praying for the strength to refuse.

But didn't she have a *duty* to put things on a better footing with Marco? The small, Judas voice niggled at the back of her brain. Hadn't the time come to put other people's needs before her own? Ben would find out the truth one day...

'*Scusi*, Signor Daretta...' A maid had appeared behind Marco. '*Telefono.*'

There was a rapid exchange in Italian which Polly couldn't follow. Marco was frowning. Then he shrugged.

'Excuse me, Polly. I'll come straight back,' he said.

She watched him weave his way through the crowds and disappear into the house. Then she sat down again, staring at her wine, unable to move, oddly paralysed by a sensation of impending catastrophe. This visit to Italy was going wrong already, and she'd only been here a few hours. She should never have come. She should have resisted her father's pressure. Damn it, Sophy should have been the one to come. She was mad, quite mad to have risked it...

She was so preoccupied, she jumped when Marco appeared in front of her.

'It's for you.' His deep voice held a dry, quizzical note which made her stare at him in confusion. 'As far as I can make out.'

'What?' She stood up so quickly she nearly collided with him. 'Who is it?' The uneasiness had taken shape, become an acute premonition.

'A child,' he said flatly.

He was watching her, watching the way the blood drained from her face, then surged back in a crimson tide of panic. 'I've just had an interesting chat with a very precocious and intelligent-sounding boy who tells me his name is Benedict Hamilton, aged three and a half.'

Polly had ceased to notice Marco's wry expression, stopped worrying about what he thought. All she was aware of as she began to blunder towards the house was a blind, gut-wrenching anxiety.

Benedict—if something had happened to Ben... But if he was actually ringing her himself, he couldn't be hurt or lying in hospital, could he? Her throat had dried, her palms felt damp, her stomach churned with fear.

Marco had caught up with her, taking her arm, steering her through the crowds. By the time he led her into a large, airy study, overlooking lawns on a different side of the house, she was trembling with the effort to stay cool and self-possessed.

'The phone's on the desk,' Marco informed her expressionlessly. 'And if you want to call him back to save his telephone bill, feel free. It's the least I can do to make up for monopolising his *mummy's* time, don't you agree, Polly?'

CHAPTER TWO

'BEN?' She knew her voice sounded strained. She was willing her heart to stop thudding. 'Mummy's here, sweetheart. Are you all right?'

''Course I'm all right. Who's the nice man?'

Polly looked over her shoulder. Marco was sitting, legs stretched out, on a low, terracotta-coloured armchair by a wide exterior doorway which was open onto the gardens. He was regarding her steadily, unsmilingly. His intent gaze made her stomach hollow.

'The...the nice man is my cousin, Marco. Now I want to know why you're ringing me, darling. Is everything okay at Janie's?'

'Yup. Bonny's got puppies, Mummy. I want the yellow one with the pink nose. Can you hear him? He's chewing my foot.'

She became conscious of a yapping in the background, and smiled involuntarily. With some relief she pictured her small son, importantly holding the telephone in the family room at Janie and Will's rambling village house in Devon, probably standing on a chair to reach it, and frowning into the receiver as he was prone to do when concentrating. Bonny, she knew, was Janie and William's good-tempered golden Labrador. William was the local GP, and Janie was his wife and Polly's business partner, who'd eagerly offered to take care of Ben while Polly went to Italy...

The excitement in Ben's sweet baby voice made her smile. She never ceased to marvel at the forwardness of her son's development; at nearly three and a half, he could hold a completely intelligent conversation with most adults. Janie was convinced it was because he'd had his mother's undivided, besotted attention since birth...

'Ben, can I speak to Janie?'

'Yup...*Janie?*'

Polly eased the receiver a little further from her ear. There was

25

a pause, with some rattling noises and talking in the background, then Janie's warm, laughing voice came on the line.

'Never worry about the capacity of your son's lungs, Polly.'

'I know.' Polly visualised her friend's smiling brown eyes and mop of curly brown hair, and was instantly reassured that Ben was in safe hands. 'He could put megaphone manufacturers out of business.' She laughed quickly. 'Is everything all right, Janie?'

'Everything's fine. I didn't realise Ben had used the telephone until I went to ring someone from the kitchen extension! He must have found your contact number on the pad by the phone. You hear of young geniuses reading the *Guardian* before they're out of trainer pants, but you don't actually believe it until you spend time with one. Looking after a gifted three-year-old is proving entertaining, to say the least!'

'Well, I hope he's not driving everyone mad. I'll come back as quickly as I can.'

'You'll do no such thing! Stay longer; take a break! Will was telling me he hadn't had such fun in ages. In fact, I think he's getting broody again...'

'Really?' Polly smiled, briefly wondering if Janie's husband, a fortyish country doctor could possibly be described as broody—even if he did have a soft spot for children.

'And your father seems very keen on your peace mission,' Janie added. 'I saw him today—he popped in to see Ben. How's it going, by the way?'

'All right...' Polly hesitated, unsure how much to say. With Marco in the room, listening to every word, she could hardly confide in Janie.

Confusion was making her head spin. She squeezed her eyes shut for a second, trying to channel her thoughts. She was in an impossible situation and she had no idea how to resolve it. Except that running away probably wasn't the ideal solution now. She should have the courage to stay a little longer, try to find some way...some kind of compromise. She took a firm grip on her wayward emotions and forced herself to speak normally.

'As...as a matter of fact I *was* wondering whether to stay another night, but if you've got a new litter of puppies to look after as well...'

'Bonny's got them under control, and the weather's warm—they sleep in the old conservatory at the back. No trouble at all...'

'Well, you're superwoman, that's all I can say, and heaven knows how much this call is costing you.'

'A small fortune, no doubt, but don't hang up...Ben's itching to talk to you again...'

'I gather he wants one of Bonny's puppies?'

'Mmm. I said I'd have to talk to you about it when you get back.'

'Very diplomatic.' Polly grinned.

Ben came back on the line and entertained her with an inimitable account of his numerous activities over the last twenty-four hours. She tried to clamp down on the anxiety that consumed her while they were apart. She adored Ben so much, she dreaded turning into one of those neurotic, over-protective mothers in a few years' time. The kind who hung themselves around their sons' necks like millstones, refusing to let them go...

When Polly replaced the receiver a few minutes later, the silence in the study was deafening. In stark, potent contrast to the light-hearted warmth of her telephone conversation, the unspoken tension between herself and Marco seemed to stretch on indefinitely, until even the ticking of the carriage clock on the chimney-piece sounded like someone hammering on the wall.

'It seems I have an apology to make,' Marco said at last.

She stared at him, her throat drying again.

'You do?' Her heart was thudding like a piston. 'Why?'

He stood up and came across the room. She felt rooted to the spot beside the leather-topped desk. When he stopped in front of her, she found she was holding her breath. His height struck her suddenly as overpowering.

'I joked earlier that you weren't the maternal type, Polly. Clearly I was even more...out of date...than I thought. You appear to be a competent, caring mother.' The lidded gaze flicked to her left hand, and then lifted slowly to her white face. 'With no husband?'

'No.' She wondered if she were about to pass out. The force of tension invading her whole body was making her feel sick.

'No husband. I'm an independent woman,' she added, with an attempt at flippancy.

'Your choice or his?'

'Sorry...?' She stared up at him in mounting confusion.

Marco was regarding her with shadowed eyes.

'The father? It's Paul, I presume?'

She felt the colour seeping back into her cheeks.

'Who does he take after? Does he have blond hair, like you?' he persisted huskily. 'Or does he take after Paul?'

'Marco, I—'

'Paul has red hair, doesn't he?' He smiled mirthlessly. 'I asked Sophy once. I guess I was curious to visualise the guy you walked out on me for...'

She clenched her hands at her sides. The room was tilting menacingly around her. She wanted to lie down on the floor, curl up into a foetal ball and shut out the unbearableness of this situation...

'To describe what happened as...as my walking out on you is ridiculous, and you know it. It was a...a one-off. You didn't want to know. And I don't want to talk about this,' she told him carefully. 'It's really...none of your business, Marco.'

'Probably not.' He held her gaze, his lips twisting grimly. 'But I'm interested, all the same. You're family, Polly.'

'Don't start that again!' she said sharply. 'We're not even blood cousins, and you talk as if we were brother and sister, Marco!'

His gaze had narrowed to a dangerous dark blue glitter between thick black lashes. There was a charged silence.

'If we had been, I'd like to think that what happened between us in Cambridge would not have happened.'

She was hot all over. 'Quite,' she managed, through her teeth.

His gaze moved slowly up and down her body as she stood in front of him, sending shivers of awareness to every silent nerve-end.

'But there was nothing rational or premeditated about what did happen, was there, Polly?' His wide mouth twisted slightly. 'Speaking personally, I'm not sure I could have stopped myself at the time...'

She gave a short, angry laugh, willing her colour to fade.

'Meaning I was to blame, with my amoral, siren-like behaviour?'

Marco's face was hard to read. He stared at her in silence for a few moments.

'Not at all,' he corrected her softly. 'We have already discussed this. If you recall, I took the blame.' He moved abruptly, widening the space between them. 'Enough of the past. Let's talk about the present, Polly. How come I knew nothing about your son?'

A flare of anger made her catch her breath.

'How come you didn't know?' she echoed. Her voice shook with suppressed emotion. 'Why should you?'

'Sophy could have told me,' he countered, his voice husky.

'Yes, presumably she could, but why would she think you'd be remotely interested?'

Marco was silent again. He leaned back against the edge of the desk, his hands deep in the pockets of his jacket. His position drew attention to the lean thrust of his hips, the muscles of his thighs where the fabric of his suit stretched tight.

She looked quickly away, but not before she knew Marco had seen her looking. Her face felt hot; her brain was racing in confusion.

'You didn't tell her what happened between us, did you?' she blurted, suddenly horrified at the thought.

'I'm not in the habit of broadcasting details of my personal life,' he said in a withering voice. 'You didn't waste much time, did you, Polly? You were a virgin that night in Cambridge. A virgin on the Pill, as you assured me. Then you went off to America with Paul and stopped taking the Pill, I assume?'

Her face felt so hot, she knew she must have blushed deeply.

'Marco...please!'

'Do you live with him? Is that who you've left your son with?'

'No...' Fielding Marco's interrogation was making her brain feel woolly and uncoordinated. With a conscious effort, she managed a cool shrug. 'Paul and I don't live together.'

'Is there someone else?'

'I am not discussing my private life with you, Marco...'

'You look after your son alone?'

'Yes...no...I have good friends...' She hesitated, then went on quickly, 'Paul and I are still...close. He lives in the village—he teaches at the local primary school.'

'How cosy. He takes turns at parenting, does he? You think that is sufficient to give this little son of yours a father figure?' Marco mused caustically. 'Children should be raised in a stable relationship.'

'Of course they should—in principle.' She was outraged at his air of cool condemnation. 'Please don't patronise me, Marco! I've made the best of the situation. I love my son. He's getting everything he needs...'

'Except a full-time father, by the sound of it. And what about you?' He switched tack abruptly. The expression in his eyes sent fresh shivers down her spine. 'Are *you* getting everything you need? From this half-hearted commitment from a man who cannot even shoulder the responsibility for his own son?'

'I'm quite...happy with the way things are.'

'I cannot imagine you are happy with such a tepid arrangement,' he said huskily. 'Unless you've managed to suppress that passionate nature of yours?'

'What are you talking about?' She felt hot all over.

'Didn't you have a passionate nature, Polly?'

'Not particularly, no...'

'No? Would you like me to remind you?'

She put her hands involuntarily to her ears.

'Stop it!' she hissed. 'Why are you doing this, Marco?'

'Doing what?' He'd moved closer, decreasing the space between them to a few inches. She felt as if every nerve in her body was quivering at his nearness. 'Speaking the truth?'

'Marco, I—' She stopped. Marco was slowly but purposefully gathering her into his arms and against the strength of his body. She caught her breath to protest again, but he smothered it, his mouth hard and demanding on hers. She struggled furiously. Then abruptly his kiss became warm, gentle and coaxing.

She involuntarily parted her lips and kissed him back. She tasted the intimate thrust of his tongue, felt his powerful shudder of desire. The raw response blanked all thought from her mind.

The past rushed back. All she was aware of was Marco's hard body against hers, the luxurious feeling of being in his arms, held tightly against him, the sparks of hot desire stinging through her...

'Polly...' His voice was hoarse. With a jerky movement he grasped her hand and brought it to the centre of his chest, covering her fingers with his own. She could feel the erratic thudding of his heart. It seemed to vibrate through her own bloodstream. Her breathing was uneven. She tried to pull her hand away but he trapped it with his, linking their fingers together, palm to palm, his eyes bright beneath lowered lids.

'Stop it,' she said, fighting him blindly, her voice breaking. 'What's the point, Marco?'

'The point? To prove something to you,' he said, crushing her against him, his mouth dropping to hers again.

His tongue probed deeper, fencing with hers, taking possession of her mouth. He kissed her with a fierce, sensual hunger, and Polly trembled under the onslaught. By the time he broke away, his chest jerking as he fought for control, she was truly on fire for him.

'So what have you proved?' She felt near to tears.

'God knows,' he said. 'That you still want me? Even though you chose to go away and have a baby with another man?'

She felt her jaw drop. Waves of unreality made her sway where she stood.

'*What?*'

'Isn't that what you did?'

She shut her mouth. Careful, Polly, a voice reminded her. The effect of the last few minutes, and the irony, the injustice of this accusation, had made her blurt out her protest unthinkingly.

'You make it sound as if *I* rejected *you*...!'

'Didn't you?' he said. 'How else would you describe it, Polly? How else would you describe walking out on me in Cambridge and flying off to America with a boyfriend a few days later?'

They stared at each other blankly. Polly dropped her eyes from Marco's and turned to walk slowly over to one of the chairs by the wide doorway.

Abruptly, she sat down. She'd avoided going home after that

weekend in Cambridge. She'd gone back to Norwich, finished the last couple of days of her university year, then she'd dumped all her gear at Paul's house in London and they'd flown out to their vacation jobs working in a summer camp near Salinas, in California. She'd told her father that it was too much hassle getting all the way from East Anglia to Devon. But the real reason had been that she'd been so consumed with guilt she hadn't felt able to face Sophy.

'Well, as it turns out,' said Marco bluntly, flaying her with his cynical tone, 'maybe your behaviour saved me from making the biggest mistake of my life.'

'Which was?'

'Mistaking your teenage curiosity for genuine emotion.'

She felt the blood rush to her face. His derision sparked a flare of temper.

'*Genuine emotion?* I wonder if you'd recognise ''genuine emotion'' if you came across it, Marco! What...what possible right have you to make me feel any worse about what happened that night in Cambridge? It was just a dreadful mistake, something which happened that never should have happened...'

Marco's face paled.

'Is that how you really saw it, Polly?'

'How else could I see it?' she shot back unsteadily. 'I wasn't thinking straight; I doubt if I was even seeing straight...' The defensive words poured out, unchecked. She stopped, breathing fast, aware that the shadowy expression in his eyes had darkened and hardened.

'Obviously,' he said, after a taut silence, 'you couldn't have been seeing straight or thinking straight to allow yourself to be seduced by a *Daretta*. And I'm quite sure the rest of your family would agree that you had a lucky escape.'

Marco walked to the door.

'Excuse me, Polly. I have some telephone calls to make. Stay here. I'll be back...'

Left alone, she sat there, stunned and reeling, staring at the closed door. The telephone calls must be private, she decided wearily, since there was a telephone sitting right here on the desk. She glanced round the study, slowly taking in the bare, varnished stone walls, the polished floorboards strewn with rugs, the woven curtains in stripes of rusty-red which echoed the Tuscan earth around them. It was a lovely room, decorated with a fresh simplicity; the whole house seemed warm and welcoming.

But she shouldn't meekly stay here just because Marco had said so. However, she felt too drained for the small rebellion of disappearing. Her mind felt blank. She closed her eyes and tried to make sense of it all.

She wasn't sure exactly what Marco's apparent bitterness meant. One thing she did know, though, was not to allow herself any wildly romantic notions of a major passion thwarted by an unfortunate misunderstanding. Marco had made his feelings quite clear in his college room that evening four years ago, just before he walked out of the room and left her feeling about half an inch tall. He'd been disgusted with himself, and with her, and she'd lost no time in leaving, to put as much distance between them as she could. What would he be feeling now, if he knew the whole truth?

She opened her eyes again, staring at the peaceful scene framed in the open arch of the doorway. The distant sound of chatter and laughter from the christening guests on the terrace faded as she thought back, in some confusion, to that particular weekend.

It had been a Summer Ball; she'd been at university in Norwich, but she'd gone across to Cambridge at the invitation of a girlfriend reading medicine. Marco, although she hadn't known it beforehand, had been there as a visiting graduate—his old college even retained rooms for their alumni. One of the group of medical students they'd met up with—a guy called Ruan—had taken a strong fancy to Polly. He'd been pleasant enough physically, she recalled, blond and quite tall and muscular, but she hadn't been attracted to his personality at all. His air of sneering debauchery had been off-putting. The more he'd flirted and persisted, the more he'd pressured her to come up to his room with him, the more she'd tried to laugh it off and stick with the crowd.

Then abruptly, after only a glass and a half of champagne—though she'd felt as if she'd drunk an entire magnum to herself—

she'd found herself in a dark corner of the thirteenth-century quadrangle, oblivious to the beauty of the warm June evening and inexplicably unable to cope with Ruan's hands seeking her bare flesh at the plunge neck of her ballgown. Her head had been swimming alarmingly, her eyes struggling to focus.

By that point in the evening she hadn't even realised that Marco was at the Ball. She hadn't seen him since the Easter before she'd started university, when she and Sophy had gone to Italy at Aunt Ruth's invitation and accompanied the Daretta family to Sicily.

But, he'd told her later, he'd seen her through the crowds, and he'd been watching her erratic, lurching exit from the marquee and felt concerned about her. He'd questioned the friends she'd been with, then followed them outside, and while he'd tackled Ruan Polly had slid, apparently very gracefully, her friends told her afterwards, down the wall and into a comatose heap on the grass.

The next day—or to be more accurate, the next evening, since she'd slept until about 8.00 p.m.—still woozy-headed and disorientated, she'd found herself to be semi-naked beneath the sheets, her black taffeta ballgown hung tidily on a hanger on the back of the door.

When Marco, in jeans and a checked shirt, a cup of tea in his hand, appeared in her vision, she'd just stumbled back from the bathroom, after attempts to revive herself with a shower and some of Marco's toothpaste, and collapsed into bed again. She remembered lying there in his bed, feeling agitated, shaky and anxious. Her brain had felt numb. It had been disturbing and frightening to realise that she remembered nothing at all of the last twenty-four hours.

She'd felt terrified, trying wildly to remember what she'd done the night before. From cryptic comments that Marco made it was clear that he imagined that, as a naive first-year student trying to impress her peer group, she'd experimented with smoking some illegal substance which had combined with the alcohol and caused a dramatic adverse reaction.

The unfairness of this had been the final straw. She'd started to cry, then to shake uncontrollably. As far as she could recall, the idea that Marco thought she was stupid enough to indulge in sufficient champagne to make her pass out, and, even worse, to combine it with cannabis, which she'd never touched in her life, had been almost as upsetting as the blank gaps in her memory of what precisely had happened since she'd sipped her second glass of champagne at the Ball...

Marco had come to sit beside her on the bed, his face bleak. He'd pulled her gently into his arms. He'd begun talking, trying to reassure her, apologising for sounding moralistic. He was tired. He wasn't thinking straight. He'd been worried. He'd lain awake beside her all night, on a sleeping bag on the floor, in case she'd become ill and needed help. This husky admission had sent a warm tug of gratitude right through her body.

At some point during this part of the proceedings, the sheets had become dislodged and she'd found herself half-naked in Marco's arms. She'd become abruptly aware that the expression in his eyes, as he'd looked down at her naked breasts, full and high and tipped with tight tawny nipples which had contracted with emotion, had changed from chivalrous comforter to something very different—something darker and hungrier and much more intense...

Whereupon she'd experienced a kind of watershed after all those years of infatuation and admiration for her older cousin—an infatuation which had intensified, secret and unrequited, during that week in Sicily, when she'd seen how kind and witty and intelligent and funny he was, even though he'd been gravitating towards Sophy and treating Polly as a child. Instead of being embarrassed and awkward, she'd turned naturally into the warmth of his body, wrapped her arms round his broad shoulders, and urgently tugged him into bed with her...

Polly shuddered miserably, hardly seeing the golden view from Marco's farmhouse. She couldn't imagine ever wiping that episode from her mind. Particularly the shock of Marco's reaction afterwards. Humiliation didn't even begin to describe her feelings. The horror he'd shown, claiming that he'd 'behaved like an animal', had left her speechless. If the hours of sleep hadn't cleared her fuzzy brain, the pain of Marco's rejection of her had done the job very thoroughly instead.

As for behaving like an animal... She let out her breath on a long, shaky sigh as she thought back. His damning verdict on his own behaviour couldn't have been further from the truth. Marco's lovemaking had been... Polly closed her eyes, gripped her ribs tightly. Waves of memory washed over her and left her drained and trembling inside. She'd been in a haze, not really thinking, not rationalising her actions. She'd just been giving in to a shy but primitive need, an irresistible physical attraction to the man she'd dreamed of, fantasised about for years, and who had been, miraculously, naked in bed with her and giving every indication of reciprocating her desire.

There'd been a frantic, muted urgency in their coming together—breathless with hunger, as if being entwined in the closest of embraces wasn't close enough. Mouth to mouth, breast to chest, hips crushed as one, legs wound around each other; she had been in a haze, but she could see now, vividly, the moment when he'd been poised to enter her and he'd drawn back from her momentarily, searching her face, his own face taut with passion, and she'd reached to trace her hands shakily along his jaw, and touched the beads of sweat on his upper lip and seen the dark, fierce male desire in his eyes...

Then, later, the fleeting pain, and then the indescribable pleasure and dreamlike ecstasy had all been over, and she was back in the real world, shrinking with shock and humiliation as Marco's face had grown bleak with remorse and self-reproach. He was grimly berating himself over whether he could have made her pregnant. And, because it was too late anyway, and because there seemed little point in fanning the flames of his worry, she'd bitterly told him to forget all about it, that she was on the Pill...

It was ironic, Marco now acting as if *she'd* been the one to instantly regret what happened, she reflected miserably. But perhaps time dulled accurate memory. Perhaps it was more convenient for him to look back and cast himself in the role of caring, spurned hero, and tender, concerned lover...

The click of the door made her twist round quickly. Marco had come back in. He was carrying a tray. Polly smelled aromatic coffee and saw a plate containing slices of very English-looking christening cake—no doubt Ruth's contribution to the celebrations.

'I was still hungry. And in need of caffeine,' he said, depositing the tray on the coffee table near them and looking blandly at Polly. 'I thought we could continue talking over coffee and cake.'

'If you like,' she said, lowering her eyelids to hide the telltale panic she was feeling. 'But I'm not sure what else there is to talk about, Marco,' she finished up warily.

'I'd say we have a lot of catching up to do,' he said, pouring coffee into the cups, offering cream and sugar.

'Just cream. Thanks.' She accepted the cup and took a quick sip. The strength of the dark Italian brew was reviving. She watched Marco add a spoonful of sugar to his, and leave it black. He sat down, watching her. She felt uncomfortably as if he were playing some kind of cat and mouse game with her.

'Have some of Mother's exceptional cake,' he urged, holding out the plate. Polly dutifully took a piece, and tasted it. It had a rich, dark fruity taste, and real almond paste icing, which she adored. There was something comforting about eating it. She finished it quickly, then saw that Marco was still watching her and found herself smiling at him ruefully.

'You like fruit cake,' he observed, with a faint grin. 'Me too. Especially my mother's.'

'You'll give your wife a complex when you marry,' she quipped lightly. 'If you're fixated on your mother's cooking.'

'"Fixated" is going a bit far.' He paused to take a sizeable bite of his own piece, sitting back in his chair. 'I appreciate my mother's cooking, but I'm not a bad cook myself. Surely that's a good sign for my future wife?'

'That depends on what you can cook. Most men I've known claim to be good cooks if they can rustle up baked beans on toast.'

'You've known a lot, then?'

'Sorry?'

'A lot of men?'

She stared at him. His expression gave little away. The ink-black gaze was bland, his dark features a mask of friendly enquiry. She wished she could stop the heat from creeping into her face.

'Are we talking *biblically*?' she managed as evenly as she could. 'Do you want dates and descriptions?'

Marco's face looked drawn suddenly, his tan slightly paler. He stared at her in taut silence, then slowly drank some coffee.

'I don't expect you to itemise your sexual adventures any more than I'd itemise mine.'

'Good, Marco,' she went on heatedly, 'just because I'm a single mother doesn't give you the right to question my morals.'

He jumped to his feet suddenly, and stood there staring down at her. He thrust his hands into the pockets of his suit jacket, the expression in his eyes brooding.

'I'm not questioning your morals,' he said hoarsely. 'Polly, believe it or not, I'm just finding it hard to adjust to the fact that you have a child and nobody told me about it...'

'It just shows that...that we're not sufficiently interested in each other's lives to have kept in closer touch all this time!' she said with bitter simplicity.

'I've done my damnedest to keep in touch with you, Polly! But is that how you've felt this past four years?'

She stared up at him and caught her breath; she felt cornered, breathless, as if she were being pursued in a nightmare, unable to run.

'What do you think?'

'I don't know what to think, Polly. I suppose I should have got the message when you didn't return any of my calls, found excuses to be away from home when I came to see you and cried off at the last minute when we finally arranged to meet.' He was standing like a statue, his hands in tight fists, the blue-black gaze lidded, frightening her with its glittering focus on her face. His eyes moved downwards over her, lingering on the slight swell of her breasts at the fastening of her jacket, dropping lower to slowly take in the slender length of her thighs, where her skirt had ridden up slightly while she sat. 'But I know what I want to do right now.'

'Marco...' She was scrambling to her feet, her knees annoyingly unresponsive as she tried to straighten up to face him on a more equal basis. 'Stop this...'

'I want to take you to bed with me,' he went on huskily. 'And teach you not to play games.'

'*What?*' She could hardly breathe, her heart was hammering so violently against her ribs. 'So if there's a problem, sex is your answer?'

'In our case, maybe sex is the problem. I can't deny that I find you sexually attractive, Polly. That night in Cambridge—'

'I'm deeply flattered.' Talking about sexual attraction between them was making her stomach feel odd, her legs feel annoyingly boneless.

'That night in Cambridge, I did something I'd never done before, and I've never done since. I lost my head completely...' His mouth twisted.

She turned away from him. She was shaking.

'We both did,' she said painfully. 'But at least I found out why I passed out that night, by the way. I found out what that perverted medical student did, if you're interested...'

'I found out too. After you left,' Marco said quietly. 'He'd put a drug in your drink.'

Surprised, she turned round. She met his eyes, nodding slowly.

'How did you find out?' she asked carefully.

'I heard some students talking in the college bar. How about you?'

'My Cambridge friend found out for me. He'd got hold of something called Rohypnol. It's supposed to be used as a pre-anaesthetic medication. Apparently if you powder it and slip it into someone's drink it's tasteless, and it works like lightning. It's become notorious as the "date-rape" drug in America...'

'I felt pretty bad when I knew...' There was a bitter twist to his mouth.

'Why?' She shrugged, holding his eyes with a challenging gleam now. 'I felt a lot better when I knew the truth. I could rationalise my actions to myself. I gather that as well as being fast-acting, and causing amnesia, one of its effects is aphrodisiac—so at least that gives me an excuse for my outrageous behaviour with you the following night, doesn't it?'

There was a silence. Marco's eyes had darkened.

'As I understood it—' he spoke with dry precision '—the drug is undetectable in the bloodstream within twenty-four hours. Any aphrodisiac effects would occur earlier rather than later.'

She coloured slightly.

'Right. Point taken. Meaning that it wasn't just the Rohypnol which made me drag you into bed and touchingly offer you my virginity, Marco?'

'I guess I'd rather fool myself that you couldn't resist me.'

'Let's just say that at the time my resistance was low.'

He put his hands on her shoulders, making her jump nervously.

'Forgive me?' he urged softly. 'I've felt guilty as hell all these years...'

She stared up at him helplessly. That was why he'd been keen to meet up with her. To assuage his feeling of guilt. Her throat felt swollen with unshed tears. She nodded slightly.

'Of course I forgive you. There's nothing to forgive, Marco.'

'And you'll stay on for a while?'

She should say no. She knew she should. The atmosphere between herself and Marco was far too explosive, laced with far too much emotion for her to stay a minute longer than she had to. But something, some emotion she couldn't quite identify— guilt, perhaps, or a sense of duty towards her son—drove her to make a dangerous decision.

'All right,' she heard herself agree huskily. 'But only one more night. I have to get back. Ben's missing me. And if I've got to organise one of Janie's Labrador's puppies for him...'

'Janie?'

'My friend in the village.' She took advantage of the change of subject to ease herself free of his hands and start towards the door. 'Ben's staying with her. She helps run my genealogical agency. Her husband is the local GP. Marco, I need to...to freshen up. Can you direct me to my room...?'

'Of course.'

Acutely conscious of Marco's quiet air of triumph, now that she'd agreed to stay, she kept up a stream of inconsequential chatter as they made their way up to the first floor. She was shown into a peach-walled bedroom, the ceiling criss-crossed with old beams, gilded with afternoon sun. There were windows on two walls and dramatic views down the hillside to Florence.

'Oh, I need my cases...'

'I had them brought up for you.' Sure enough, her hand luggage and suitcase were already there, placed neatly by the bed.

'Take your time,' he advised blandly.

'Thanks. Do get back to your guests.'

As he closed the door on her she sank weakly onto the bed, her fingers snatching convulsively at the dark red rough-weave bedspread. Inside she was churning with nerves and self-disgust. She shouldn't have agreed to stay. And she should have told him the truth, she lashed herself silently. How many opportunities had there been for her to say, quite simply, Ben is your son?

She was a coward, a liar, and she despised herself.

But she'd despise herself just as much if she destroyed Sophy's relationship with Marco. And surely if Marco loved Sophy it could only hurt both Ben and herself if she allowed him to get involved in their lives...

CHAPTER THREE

POLLY woke very early the next morning. It was her own fault. Having chosen not to close the shutters last night, she'd lain and watched the moon, high and cold in the black sky. Now the sky was hazy blue, and the sun was flooding in. A clinking, chopping sound from outside suggested a gardener at work.

Swinging her legs out of bed, she sat up and placed her bare feet on the polished wooden floor. She blinked, yawned, stared down at her feet beneath the hem of her cream cotton nightdress.

Her toes were in a warm patch of sun. Still sleepy, she felt a hazy tug of happiness. She tried to work out why. She recognised these feelings from early childhood; she felt loved, protected. Safe. Feelings she hadn't enjoyed since Mum had died and Dad had married again, to Sophy's mother, and Sophy's arrival in the family had subtly rocked her secure little world...

But to wake up this morning feeling safe? Even as the aftermath of some kind of dream this struck a jarring note as her present predicament flooded back. Ben's surprise telephone call, Marco's reaction—all yesterday's stressful half-truths and evasions.

She'd rung and spoken to Janie again last night, without the tension of Marco's presence, and been teasingly reassured that Ben was fine, and being absolutely no trouble whatsoever, and that she could stay in Italy as long as she liked. Which had been one less worry, admittedly.

But she must be crazy to feel safe, she reflected, chewing her bottom lip. Let alone happy. Where had that come from? From being with Marco again, a niggling voice informed her. Which meant that she was even crazier.

Watching the moon last night, she'd thought about Ben, back in England, and about the last four years of her life. She'd looked at the photograph of him which she kept tucked in her address book and blinked back tears, missing him and hoping he was tucked up in bed and safe and happy, and she'd fallen asleep with a hazy and improbable vision of how life might have been...*if.*

If...that tiny word which tortured so effectively.

If she'd told Marco she was pregnant, instead of taking that lonely, heart-wrenching decision to go it alone. *If* she'd told Marco when she'd given birth to Ben...

She'd fallen asleep last night imagining herself, Ben and Marco—the three of them—doing family things together, like playing on the beach, or going to the cinema, or swimming, or horseriding. Or simply sitting round the fire together, toasting teacakes, playing Ludo...

Maybe that was why she'd woken up feeling so idiotically happy. The dream had lingered for a few moments before evaporating into reality...

She went to the bathroom and took a quick shower, and washed her hair. Washing her hair usually helped her to pull her thoughts together.

This morning it didn't.

She needed air. She'd go for an early-morning walk.

Donning white canvas jeans, pumps and a pale yellow T-shirt, she pulled her hair into a chaotic ponytail and darted downstairs.

Outside the French doors, the fragile scent of late wisteria floated down from the farmhouse walls, heady and euphoric. She stood still and closed her eyes, breathed in the fresh scents of the early Tuscany morning.

'Couldn't you sleep?'

Marco's smiling voice made her eyes fly open. She stared up at him as he stood there in front of her, in faded denim shirt, indigo jeans and deck shoes, his black hair still damp from washing, a wedge falling forward over his eyes.

'I slept like a log. The sun woke me. I had to come out for a walk...'

'Come and have breakfast with me first,' he invited.

She followed his gaze across the terrace. A table was laid for breakfast—white cloth, olive-green pottery, yellow napkins—in a sunny corner beneath the wisteria-covered pergola.

'Okay.' She shrugged, and went across slowly and sat down.

There was a basket of rolls, warm beneath a napkin, butter, some kind of jam in a small earthenware dish, a pot of coffee, a small jug of cream. She'd just realised how hungry she was. She smiled cautiously at Marco as he sat opposite.

'Do you always have breakfast this early?'

Taking a roll, he broke it open, buttered it thickly, then covered it as generously with jam. She watched his hands as he did this; she couldn't help herself. Marco's hands were beautiful, lean and brown. She found herself longing for him to touch her, the longing so forceful her stomach felt hollow with need.

'I'm an early riser—I usually go for a run before breakfast.' He took a large bite and chewed, watching her through narrowed eyes. 'But this morning was earlier than normal—I couldn't sleep last night.'

She made a show of buttering her own roll before answering, addressing her entire attention to the task.

'I'm sorry to hear that. You're not ill?' She knew her voice sounded stilted.

'No. I'm not ill. I just have things on my mind. Do you want some coffee?'

'Please.' There was an uneasy silence as he poured hers with cream and took his own black. Polly added some jam to her roll and took a small bite.

The jam was apricot, her favourite. She ate slowly, thinking about last night. She'd let Marco call the airline for her, since her Italian was sketchy. But, having listened to her insistence that she could only stay one more night, he'd returned with the cavalier announcement that he'd delayed her flight until the end of the week.

She'd greeted this news with inner confusion. Secretly joyful at the idea of spending so much longer in his company, she'd nevertheless protested that she couldn't stay that long. 'Treat yourself to a break,' he'd advised calmly, with that determined glitter in his eyes which made her uneasy all over again.

Marco was watching her now, smiling faintly as she demolished another roll in preoccupied silence.

'This is very cosy,' he commented, when the silence had

stretched out. 'Just the two of us, eating breakfast together, like an old married couple.' His tone was gently ironic.

'Hardly.' The defensive retort came out more sharply than she'd meant it to.

'True. You're twenty-three; I'm only thirty-one. So we're not exactly old. We're not married. And we're not even a couple.'

'Quite.' She felt her whole body growing warm beneath her clothes at the expression in his eyes. 'In fact, we don't even know each other very well, do we, Marco?' she finished up, with a light, brittle laugh.

'Possibly not.'

'How could we know each other well? How often have we actually met, would you say? In our entire lives?' she persisted, drinking some coffee. She watched his eyes narrow, and recollected too late that she'd dodged meeting him on several occasions over the past four years. She felt herself colouring. She already knew precisely how many times they'd met. Each occasion was etched indelibly in her memory.

Marco met her eyes with a glitter in his.

'Three,' he told her flatly. 'When you were thirteen, I bumped into you—literally—at Hamilton Priory. When you were eighteen, you came to Sicily with us that Easter. And when you were nineteen, we met by chance at the Ball in Cambridge.'

'What a memory,' she murmured, reluctantly impressed by his powers of recall.

'For all my faults, I have an excellent memory. I remember every detail of our meetings, Polly.' He inspected the spiral of steam rising from his cup, then glanced up at her with a wry look in his eyes. 'Even down to my first impression of you on the steps of Hamilton Priory that day.'

'Which was?'

'Frightened rabbit.'

'Thanks!' She glared at him and put down her coffee cup with a clatter.

He grinned unrepentantly. 'You had your hair in a plait, you were wearing a brace on your teeth, and you looked up at me like you thought I was the devil incarnate.'

'I did not! And how you can remember such details, from ten years ago, I can't imagine!'

'Like I said, I have a good memory.'

'Obviously. You shocked me, that's all—you came bursting out of the house, and I was so surprised I stopped dead and nearly got flattened by the paperboy...'

'And I gallantly saved you from serious injury.'

'True.' She smiled slightly. 'But you looked so ferocious and violent I'd have thought you were a...a criminal burgling the place, if Aunt Ruth hadn't followed you out.'

'Ironic,' he murmured, a hint of coolness in his voice now, 'since that was the gist of your grandmother's comment just before I stormed out...'

'She called you a criminal?' Polly felt her stomach contract with shock.

'Words to that effect.' Marco's mouth twisted. 'Except that she used my Sicilian ancestry as a more satisfactory insult...'

Polly stared at him, round-eyed with horror. She'd known about the family feud, but the finer details had never come to light before now.

'In what way?' she enquired cautiously.

'Don't act the innocent, Polly. Surely you know in what way? My father was born in a notorious town in Sicily,' he explained flatly. 'When my mother chose to marry him, it wasn't just his lowly trade that offended your family. It was the stigma of his birthplace. Don't pretend you never knew the cause of the family feud.'

She bleakly shook her head.

'Surely Granny Hamilton didn't seriously think...?'

Marco's expression was coolly cynical as he looked at her.

'My mother upset the Hamilton clan by marrying my father. He was too poor, he came from Sicily, and he'd got her pregnant. They cut all contact with her from the moment she left home. My mother had gone to see your grandmother that day, hoping to heal the rift. She thought that because my father had been successful—rising from being a humble chef to owner of a chain of pizza restaurants, managing to pay for my education at a top English public school—her stepmother might have softened in her attitude. Instead, the old lady accused my father of gaining his wealth through illegal means. The idea that he could have achieved success through a legitimate business apparently didn't cut any ice with her. She went on to suggest that despite my studying for a law degree at Cambridge I was destined to follow in his footsteps. Either by becoming a "waiter in a cheap café", as she put it, or else going into the "other family business"—presumably as a gangster.'

Polly put down her roll, half eaten. She felt physically sick.

'Marco, I honestly never knew...'

'The family feud speaks for itself, Polly,' he pointed out quietly. 'Why else do you think the older generations of the Hamiltons and the Darettas have stayed estranged all these years? I've tried to let it all wash over me, but it's been difficult. Particularly bearing in mind the profession I'm in, and the kind of scum I deal with in court on a regular basis...'

'But my father couldn't have—' She stopped, a wave of heat colouring her face. She'd been about to say that her father couldn't possibly have agreed with Granny Hamilton, couldn't possibly have been so ridiculously prejudiced. But precisely how had her father felt about the Daretta clan? He was a quiet, reserved man. He tended to keep his feelings to himself. She couldn't remember his ever having expressed such an extreme opinion as Granny Hamilton's, but neither had he made any effort to mend fences with Aunt Ruth—his stepsister—and her husband, Tino...

Until this christening, she reflected. In spite of her resistance, her list of excuses for not being able to go, Dad had been visibly upset at his prior court commitments and had pressed her to accept the invitation...

'I have a suggestion,' Marco said abruptly, watching her. 'The past is too contentious. Let's leave it alone for now. If we don't feel we know each other very well, let's make the most of your extended stay here, Polly.'

'How do you suggest we do that, Marco?'

'We'll go out for the day,' he suggested, his eyes warming at the wary smile on her lips. 'We'll go down to Florence, see if we can beat the queues to get into the Uffizi or the Bargello, if not we'll skip culture and be decadent, and drink cappuccino in the Piazza della Signoria. We'll have lunch by the river, and dinner up at a little restaurant where they do the best pasta Napolitana I've tasted...'

'What about all your house-guests?'

'I just provided the house. They're Mother's and Marietta's guests. And Mother's in charge, just the way she likes to be.' He made a comical face and Polly laughed. 'Most of them have to leave first thing after breakfast in any case. We won't even be missed. What do you think?'

Suddenly, irrationally, she felt caution fading in the knowledge that Marco seemed to want to spend a whole day in her company.

'It sounds wonderful,' she agreed, flushed with cautious pleasure.

'Great. How soon can you be ready?'

Polly drained her coffee cup and stood up.

'Give me ten minutes,' she said simply.

It was a magical day. Looking back, there was no clue to the anguish in store for her, no hint of the drama about to unfold and tear her world apart when she returned.

The drive down to Florence, in Marco's silver-blue soft-top Aston Martin, was through flower-filled villages, the sun warm on her face in the open car. True to her word, she'd kept her preparations simple, swopping the T-shirt for a short, loose amber silk blouse, which skimmed the waist of the white jeans, and changing the pumps for flat tan loafers. She grabbed a cashmere sweater in a darker shade, cleaned her teeth and brushed her hair. In less than ten minutes she was down in the courtyard, sunglasses and tan leather shoulder bag firmly in place, her stomach fluttering with pleasurable anticipation.

Marco was waiting for her. He wore black sunglasses, and he'd changed into a soft cotton shirt checked in Prussian blue, red and cream, with a well-worn linen jacket in a shade of faded terracotta. From then on he was effortless company: witty, relaxed, entertaining, deferring to her wishes but efficiently in charge of the day's itinerary.

Marco knew someone who let them skip the queue for the

Uffizi, and they spent a couple of hours strolling past Renaissance masterpieces she'd only ever seen in books. They pushed through growing crowds, from room to room, staring at the golden legends of Titian, Da Vinci and Botticelli, until Polly felt her head beginning to ache.

'I was supposed to be coming to Florence during my history degree,' she told Marco, as they paused in front of a fierce picture of Hercules and Antaeus, wrestling for supremacy. 'I included art history in my course...'

'In that case, forgive me for even suggesting we might give the culture a miss,' Marco grinned at her. 'I sometimes feel over-dosed on it in Italy. Haven't they got a bronze sculpture of this—' he pointed at the Hercules painting '—in the Bargello?'

'I think so...' She consulted the guidebook and nodded. 'Shall we call it a day here, and move on?'

'Lunch first.'

'Definitely.' She smiled at him in relief.

They sat outside in the sunshine, watching the crowds and the agile, weaving waiters, church bells ringing out and sending a flock of doves fluttering overhead from their dovecote high in the tower. They ate a relaxed meal beneath a striped sun umbrella, and talked about art and history. She was surprised at his depth of knowledge.

'You seem to know a lot about the history of art, for a lawyer,' she pointed out teasingly.

'I don't read dusty law books all the time.'

'Obviously. I'm impressed.'

'You did well to find yourself a career connected with your love of history.' Marco was leaning back in his chair, having demolished parma ham and melon, and buttered tagliatelle with tomato and oregano. 'I suppose you didn't manage to finish your degree course?'

Polly finished her own tagliatelle and put her spoon and fork back in the dish.

'You're right, I didn't,' she agreed slowly. 'But we agreed we wouldn't talk about that.'

'So we did.' Marco's dark face was wry. 'Tell me about your life in England, Polly. How do you cope?'

'I cope very well. Dad's around, of course, although I don't lean on him much because he's far too busy in court to help much with Ben. But I'm really lucky to have Mary, a woman from the village, who comes in every day to help in the house. She loves children and brings her little nephews and nieces sometimes to play, and she adores Ben. And Janie helps a lot, with The Family Tree and with Ben.'

'The Family Tree?' He smiled. 'That's what you call your business?'

'Yes. Do you like the name?'

'Very good. So you're the proprietor of The Family Tree, tracing people's ancestors. How do you spend your leisure time?'

'Very boringly, I'm afraid. I'm the secretary of the local History Society. And I go to yoga once a week. That's about it, really, as far as personal leisure time goes. But I do lots of things with Ben. I go swimming with him. And we walk a lot, on the beach, the cliffs—you know, watching the birds, looking up the names of wild flowers, and shells and...that kind of thing...'

'A crazy social whirl.'

'I'm quite happy.'

He looked at her for a few moments, his eyes unreadable.

'I'm sure you are, Polly.'

'Don't make that sound so patronising.'

His gaze darkened.

'I didn't mean to. Believe it or not, hearing someone claim such homely pleasures in life makes a refreshing change.'

'Perhaps I should add ''Anna'' to my name by deed poll?'

His slight smile echoed hers, but she wasn't sure if he remembered what she was referring to. Probably not. He wouldn't recall how he'd dubbed her 'Pollyanna', and consigned her to kindergarten status in one teasing moment during that visit to Sicily, five years ago.

Whereas she had never forgotten. She and Sophy had gone, at Aunt Ruth's invitation, to spend the Easter holiday with them and had visited Prizzi, on Easter Sunday, to see the famous 'Dance of the Devils'.

Spending that week with the Darettas had fuelled her infatuation with Marco. No—more than that. In that week she'd fallen hopelessly in love with him. Maybe it had been seeing him on his home territory, in the heart of his family. Before that he'd been a distant figure whom she'd hero-worshipped from afar, the dark, lean, intense-looking Sicilian cousin who'd stormed out of Hamilton Priory, figuring in her imagination in all kinds of secret, girlish fantasies.

But that week in Sicily she'd seen a warm, relaxed, affectionate Marco, who was kind to his parents and played with infinite patience with his little three-year-old niece, Rosa, his elder sister's child, and who gently teased his sisters and his two English cousins.

She blushed to think how she'd cherished a photograph of the two of them, laughing together, taken at the Prizzi procession. Aunt Ruth had sent it on to her at university with a general batch of photos taken during the vacation. She'd put it in a frame and kept it by her bed. But she'd known all the time, deep down, that Marco could never be hers. It had been obvious that week in Sicily. He'd had eyes only for Sophy, with her burnished golden hair and her violet-blue eyes and stunning, model looks.

He'd treated Polly teasingly. Like a little sister. She recalled quite vividly when the 'Pollyanna' tag had started—they'd been watching the colourful Easter procession, which mimed the struggle between good and evil, and Marco had made a remark about evil sometimes being stronger than good. She'd protested that all it took was faith and a belief in the concept of a Guardian angel... Marco had laughed, then apologised for being such a cynic, and she'd earned her nickname for the rest of the week...

Then, on the last night of the holiday, after they'd all been out for a meal, she'd seen Marco and Sophy kissing in the darkness of the courtyard outside the house. She'd watched for a few appalled seconds as Sophy had writhed against him with hungry desire, her golden hair gleaming in the dark, her fingers raking into Marco's thick black hair...

Turning, and blindly stumbling away, she'd wondered miserably how simply witnessing an event could cause such a physical pain in her stomach...

'Sometimes you move in circles where it's easy to forget real values,' Marco was saying quietly. 'I envy the simple life you've just described.'

She blinked away the memories. They were leaving the past alone, she reminded herself determinedly.

'Is your life so complicated?'

He shrugged, draining his wineglass.

'I spend a lot of time in the unsavoury world of the criminal courts, and occasionally I find myself defending people I don't particularly trust; mostly I act as prosecuting counsel.'

'You're working in London at the moment, aren't you?'

He shook his head. 'Rome.'

'Oh. But, Sophy—' She stopped. She didn't want to bring Sophy into the conversation again. But her stepsister had got Marco's current location wrong, surprisingly...

'What about Sophy?'

'Nothing. It doesn't matter. Are you defending or prosecuting?'

'I was prosecuting. The case finished last week.'

She waited, but he didn't elaborate.

'What kind of case?'

'You wouldn't want to hear the nasty details,' he assured her, his mouth thinning as he smiled. 'Are we going to have coffee here? Or shall we move on virtuously to the Bargello, and reward ourselves with coffee and cakes afterwards?'

'That last suggestion sounds the best,' she laughed.

By early evening, sated by culture and the bustle of the city, they agreed that a shower and change of clothes was required before dinner. Polly leaned back in the passenger seat, tired and extremely happy, as they drove back up out of Florence.

She and Marco had talked as they'd never had a chance to talk before, and she felt closer to him than she'd ever felt, maybe just because she now knew simple things about him: how he preferred red wine to white, liked his coffee strong and black with one sugar, liked Mexican food as much as Italian, and his mother's English cooking best of all...

She knew that he shared her liking for the cinema, especially films by the Italian director Bertolucci, how he ran, swam and played tennis, went skiing in Italy and occasionally climbed and sailed in England, how he'd learned how to cook from his father, during school holidays, in the heat and noise and chaos of the pizza kitchens, how he liked to read fast-moving thrillers, had a vast CD collection ranging from the Beatles to Oasis and a collection of jazz records, including Glen Miller's entire repertoire.

'I love Glen Miller!' she'd exclaimed, laughing at his sheepish expression.

'That settles it,' he'd announced solemnly. 'I'm coming to stay, invited or not.'

She'd laughed lightly, then trailed off, caution setting in. And guilt. She'd quickly changed the subject. She had to be careful. There'd been a couple of moments during the day when they'd been getting on so brilliantly, when being in Marco's company had felt so happy, so relaxed and natural, she'd had an almost irresistible urge to blurt out the truth, to turn to him and say simply, We have a son...

The effort of keeping her secret was exhausting. And depressing.

As they drove back now, she closed her eyes and stifled an enormous yawn.

'We can go out to dinner, or eat in, if you prefer?' Marco suggested easily, as the Aston Martin swooped effortlessly up the autostrada. 'We should have the house to ourselves by now.'

'I don't mind. Whatever you want to do.' She yawned again, and smiled ruefully. 'I'm quite happy to go out if you want to. I'm sure a shower will revive me.'

'I could cook you a Tuscan speciality,' he offered, 'with local *chianina* beef and *porcini*—wild mushrooms. While you recline on a sofa with a glass of Chianti Classico, and some Italian Renaissance music to reflect our day of culture. How does that sound?'

Polly turned to look at him as he turned the car into the courtyard and cut the engine. She sat for a few moments, savouring the languorous silence all around them. The farmhouse windows were tinted ruby-red in the sunset. Even the old stone walls had taken on a rusty-red glow. In its sweeping setting of pale corn and acid-green vines and dark pointed poplars on the horizon, it looked solid and welcoming and already familiar, like home.

'Marco, how come you haven't married and settled down to that simple, homely existence you say you crave?' she teased impulsively.

He stared at her for so long she felt herself go hot.

'Why do you ask that?'

'Talking about what you're going to cook for dinner, you sound so...domesticated!' she managed lightly, her throat drying. The look in the narrowed, black-fringed eyes was unnerving suddenly.

'Every woman's ideal husband?' he enquired silkily. 'You sound just like my mother. Well, who knows? Maybe the ideal woman hasn't succumbed to my charm at the ideal time?' There was a dry note in his voice. 'I'm only thirty-one. Still time to find her. You can't hurry these things, Polly. You, of all people, should know that.'

He was referring to her single mother status, she presumed miserably.

'True,' she agreed huskily. 'I should, shouldn't I?'

She closed her eyes briefly. Time should have taught her that she wasn't Marco's ideal woman; it still hurt to hear it flatly confirmed.

'Well? What's it to be?' he prompted, his voice husky. 'Dinner out, or risk my home cooking?'

She expelled a long breath. With an effort, she turned a calm smile in his direction.

'How could I resist your home cooking?' Thinking of home, she had a sudden, overwhelming urge to ring and speak to Janie, reassure herself that Ben was all right. 'Do you mind if I telephone England, Marco?'

'Go ahead. I'll go and take a bath, then put my chef's hat on.'

Back in her room, Polly showered. Then she put on a dress, the only other outfit she'd brought for what had originally been a one-night stay. It was a cool sleeveless shirt-dress, one of her favourites, cut long and lean and belted, in a soft brick-pink linen. She slipped her feet back into the tan loafers, then changed her mind. The only other shoes she had with her were the taupe suede high heels, and on impulse she opted for those. She needed the extra confidence that the high heels gave her.

She inspected her face in the mirror. The open car trip had whipped extra life into her skin, and it was showing the beginnings of a slightly flushed pre-tan already. Even her hair looked lighter; the barley-blonde had a tendency to fade to mouse in the English winter. She put on minimal make-up: just a hint of blue-grey shadow the same colour as her eyes, a fluff of powder and some dusky-peach lipstick. She finished off with a generous spray from the bottle of Eau d'Issey that Dad had bought her for Christmas, then stared at the finished effect with mixed feelings. She was glowing with anticipation, she recognised, and felt a shiver of apprehension as well.

Today had been time out. She and Marco had pretended there were no spectres lurking in the past, and she'd loved—no, revelled in every minute of his company. And here she was now, spraying on expensive designer scent, putting on lipstick, as excited as an innocent on her first date...

With an inner groan, she sat down firmly on the chair by the bed and picked up the telephone.

To her surprise, Janie's number rang out unanswered. Chewing her lip, Polly let it ring for ages before cradling the receiver, frowning. It was six o'clock in England. The time when Ben would surely be having his bath, eating his tea, being put to bed. Anxiety gnawed at her stomach and she tried to shrug it off. If something had happened, she'd have heard. She must try not to worry so much.

The minute Marco saw her, as she emerged onto the terrace half an hour later, he raised his eyebrows at her expression.

'What's wrong, Polly?'

'Nothing, really.'

'Did you get through to whoever you wanted to speak to?'

She shook her head, gratefully accepting the glass of wine he was offering her.

'There was no reply.' She sipped the cool dry wine, forced a smile. 'I just wanted to speak to Janie—check Ben was happy. But...they've probably gone out for the day or something—a special treat to the zoo or wildlife park or...'

Marco came to sit next to her on the wicker sofa on the terrace, flustering her with his nearness. He stretched his long legs out in front of him and leaned back, turning to thoughtfully inspect her face.

'And now you're worried? You really love this little boy of yours.'

'Of course!' She was fighting down waves of heat at Marco's closeness.

'Don't worry; everything's fine.'

'Yes, I'm sure it is. I just...haven't been away from Ben much. It feels wrong, somehow.'

'I saw your face when he rang yesterday,' Marco mused. 'Are you in the habit of thinking the worst whenever anything unexpected happens?'

She sighed, and laughed slightly. 'Probably. Someone once said to me that if you're a worrier, you should never have children...'

'Is it possible you dialled the wrong number?'

'Well, I suppose it's possible...' She put down her glass of wine and reached to delve into her bag, took out her address book and leafed through to check Janie's number. 'No, I'm sure I dialled the right one...'

There was a brief pause.

'Ben wasn't exactly planned, I imagine?' Marco said quietly.

She stiffened.

'No.'

'It must have been an unpleasant shock, discovering you were pregnant.'

'The only thing I'm sure of is that I wouldn't be without Ben now, for anything in the world...'

Marco reached out and slowly took her hand.

'Polly...'

'Hmm?' Her head bent, she hoped her hot cheeks were hidden by her hair.

'Look at me...' The deep voice was huskier.

'Marco, please don't...'

'Don't what?' He used his other hand to grasp her chin, turning her face determinedly towards him, searching her eyes with his. 'Try to get closer to you?'

'Try to take advantage of convenient proximity, you mean...'

The accusation was probably unjust, she knew. Marco might dislike commitment, but to her knowledge he wasn't prone to pouncing on females just because they happened to be there. Desperation was making her defensive.

He went still for a second, his eyes hardening, a chill in the dark blue depths.

'That's what you think?' he murmured bleakly. 'Is that really what you think of me, Polly?'

She stared at him in silence. Her throat felt closed, giving her a panicky feeling of not being able to breathe.

'I don't really know what to think,' she managed finally, willing her heart to stop its dramatic thudding against her breastbone.

'Even if that were true, can you blame me?'

'What's that supposed to mean?'

'You haven't exactly been putting yourself in my proximity these last four years,' he pointed out, on a roughened laugh. 'You left Cambridge without a word. You've been avoiding me ever since. Now that I've got you here, the novelty might be going to my head.'

Then, without any warning, he bent forward and kissed her. He kissed her hard, ignoring her stiff resistance, sliding his hands up to her nape, his fingers into her hair, his thumbs tracing the edge of her jawline, smoothing up to skim the circle of her ears, until with a moan she relaxed and parted her lips. Then he grew gentler, his tongue sliding hungrily inside her mouth; physical need overtook her, making her reach unthinkingly to hold him in trembling urgency.

'Polly, sweetheart...'

Hot and confused, she gazed at him as he pulled away and stared at her. Seeing the intensity in his eyes, she felt a swirl of reaction, disturbing and disorientating, as if she were being sucked into hot darkness.

'I should know better, but I still want you so much it's driving me crazy...' He sounded wryly despairing, as if the words were dragged from him, unreservedly against his better judgement.

She felt raw with need, from her head to her toes. She was about to attempt a reply when she saw his face alter, felt him tense and move slightly away from her.

He was staring down at the floor, just in front of the sofa. She followed his gaze. Heat surged in her face when he bent, jerkily, to pick something up, and she saw what he'd found. It must have fallen out of her address book a few minutes ago...

Marco had Ben's photo in his hand, a picture of a small boy in his favourite jeans and bright red hooded tracksuit top, smiling with wide-eyed vulnerability at the camera. The photo was innocent and horribly incriminating at the same time.

She realised that Marco was looking, thunderstruck, at a tiny, exact replica of the way he would have looked twenty-eight years ago.

CHAPTER FOUR

THE silence felt like an enormous weight, pressing down on her. She was holding her breath, she realised dimly, as if suspension of breathing might delay the eruption she knew was coming. She tried to speak, but her throat seemed to have locked.

'This is Ben?' Marco's voice was ominously quiet.

She jerked her head round to look at him. His gaze was fixed on her.

'Yes. That's Ben.' Her voice sounded as if it were coming from a long way off. She clenched her hands at her sides. She was trembling.

Marco's eyes drilled into her, hard, and shadowed with bleak emotion.

'He's mine.' The raw bitterness cut her to the bone. 'Isn't he, Polly?'

She swallowed jerkily. She'd imagined a scene like this, hundreds of times, in her head. But nothing had prepared her for the reality.

'Well? Isn't he?' With an abrupt gesture of controlled violence, he put down the photograph, grasped her arms and gave her a slight shake. 'For God's sake, Polly. I have a right to know!'

Her heart was thudding like a piston. Every last vestige of saliva seemed to have been sucked from her mouth. She swallowed again, shivering convulsively. He released her and stood up, towering over her.

'I warn you,' he said flatly, 'I'll take blood tests. Don't lie to me.'

'He is your son.'

There. It was said. She'd admitted it finally; she heard the echo of her voice in the silence, flat and devoid of emotion.

The silence went on and on. Eventually, he said with chilling quietness, 'Why didn't you tell me, Polly?'

'Why do you think?'

'I'm not quite sure, but I have a few ideas,' he spat softly. 'Shall I start guessing? Is this the game, Polly? I have to come up with reasons why I think you left Cambridge without a word to me, somehow omitted to tell me I'd got you pregnant, and hid the existence of my son from me for more than three years?'

'Marco...'

'What were you afraid of? Family disapproval? Couldn't face your father and grandmother with a *Daretta* bastard growing in your belly?'

'Don't use that word! Don't you dare call my son a bastard...'

'It's accurate. It's what he is! And it's your own goddamned fault! A Hamilton conspiracy! Because anything was preferable to acknowledging a member of the notorious Daretta clan as the father. Have I guessed right?'

He watched her with narrowed eyes.

She pressed a shaking hand to her mouth, her whole body clenched in distress. She found his mounting anger frightening, but even worse was that dark, haunted look in his eyes; for a brief moment she'd glimpsed the years of painful outrage he'd felt at the Hamiltons' treatment of his mother. With a stab of anguish, she realised that he believed prejudice and snobbery to be her motive...

'No,' she whispered tightly, 'you're wrong...'

'Am I?' He strode to the edge of the terrace, swinging round to fix her with a look so potent with rage she felt her throat dry. 'So, explain the conspiracy of silence! Explain the mystery of my letters and telephone calls to you, unanswered!'

She felt her heart jolt. She'd taken a couple of wary, polite telephone calls from him, when he'd been trying to fix up a time for them to meet, but she'd never received any letters.

'What letters...?'

'Please, spare me the touching affectations of surprise!' he shot back acidly. 'That really would be the final insult, Polly!'

She shifted her position on the sofa, rubbed a hand shakily over her face. Her head felt heavy, spinning with confused information.

'Marco,' she began carefully, struggling for a sane train of thought, 'before this conversation gets any more...out of hand, just think back to...to that night in Cambridge. What happened between us was a...a spur-of-the-moment thing. Obviously neither of us were thinking straight. I...I was still groggy from that drug the night before. And...and you said you'd hardly slept all night, worrying about me... When we'd made love, you were horrified at what had happened. You made your feelings quite clear. And, bearing in mind that you were involved with my stepsister, Sophy, I couldn't blame you—'

'*Involved?*' he cut in bluntly. 'What the hell do you know about my relationship with Sophy?'

'Don't bother trying to pretend!' she bit out, goaded by his tone, 'I was there in Prizzi, remember?'

'I do remember being in Prizzi,' he said sardonically. 'The rest of your point escapes me, unfortunately.'

'You obviously have a selective memory, so I won't waste my energy arguing with you.' She matched his tone for sarcasm. He wasn't going to admit that he and Sophy were an item...maybe because he felt so guilty about making love to her that night in Cambridge, knowing he'd been betraying Sophy? Polly dragged her hand through her hair, suddenly exhausted. Did he think she was stupid? She'd seen them kissing, practically eating each other, for heaven's sake. Sophy still talked about him non-stop on the rare occasions she and Polly met up. And hadn't he admitted just yesterday that Sophy had already been out here to stay with him?

'You want to know why I didn't tell you about Ben? Because you'd have felt some kind of...of responsibility for something you wanted no part of!'

'You think I'd have wanted no part of my own *son*?'

She stared at him, her colour draining.

'He is *my* son, Marco. His conception was a mistake on your part. That's all. When...when a child is planned, conceived in love...that's different. Ben was a...a by-product of a disastrous weekend. And as far as I was concerned, your reaction in Cambridge proved your lack of interest in me, and, I assumed, him.'

The expression on Marco's face was so black she tensed in fear, convinced he was about to hit her.

'You have a twisted notion of responsibility,' he said harshly. 'You had no intention of keeping me in the picture, did you? When I said I was worried you could be pregnant, you told me you were on the Pill. That was a lie, I presume?'

She coloured.

'I had been on the Pill,' she said quietly. 'I...I'd been pre-scribed it for some menstrual problems.' She felt herself blushing even deeper, and felt impatient with herself. 'But then I stopped taking it—it didn't agree with me and I was worried about side effects; it just didn't feel right...'

'So why did you tell me you were on it?'

She stared at him in silence for a few moments.

'Because it was what you wanted to hear!' she said at last. 'Don't you think I already felt sufficiently humiliated that night? I'd just let you make love to me without really thinking about what I was doing; I was still half-doped from that drug. And then you discovered I was a virgin and exploded into a self-righteous lecture about my stupidity and your lack of self-control. All in all I realised that the wisest thing to do was extricate myself as quickly as possible! There seemed no point in worrying you un-necessarily, when it was too late anyway! So I told you I was on the Pill. To spare your *belated* concern...!'

'Very thoughtful of you,' he said drily. 'Then you disappeared to America with your boyfriend, and when you came back you contrived to be in some other part of the country when I came to see you, and you ignored my letters.'

She stared at the floor. The heat washing over her now was different; it wasn't embarrassment, it was anger.

'I didn't actually get any letters,' she told him quietly. She could feel her stomach contracting with mounting indignation.

'So...presumably someone intercepted them,' Marco mused bleakly.

She shrugged slowly. Inside, she churned with a sick sense of betrayal. Was it possible that someone had really taken letters addressed to her? Who? Her father? She recoiled from the idea...

'Ah, well—' he sounded bitterly amused '—that's life, I guess.

However, what was to stop you from picking up a telephone? Or putting pen to paper?'

She gave a shuddering sigh.

'I just told you, Marco. I thought you didn't want to know. And I certainly didn't want you shouldering your "responsibilities" out of duty!'

He gazed at her in simmering silence.

'Well, that's the only compliment I've had so far.' He smiled mirthlessly. 'At least you had the perception to realise that if I knew I'd fathered a child, I would "shoulder my responsibilities"! Better late than never, I guess. My son will be flying out to Italy and acquiring Italian citizenship as fast I can get the papers organised...'

'I beg your pardon...?'

'You heard. My son has spent his first years in England. Now he is coming to Italy, where he belongs.'

'What...what if your son's *mother* wishes him to remain in England?'

His gaze was shadowed as he raked his eyes from her head to her toes.

'What you want right now doesn't come into it...' he advised her huskily.

'How can you possibly say that...?'

'Because you've lied to me, deliberately excluded me from what should have been the most memorable period of my life.' His voice cracked slightly and he paused for a moment, breathing raggedly. 'Ben is my son. He is a Daretta. He's been deprived of his father. He needs to spend time here, now. With me.'

She watched in disbelief as he turned on his heel and walked, slightly unsteadily, back into the house.

She stood still, trembling with shock, for several minutes. Then, her heart heavy, she went inside after him.

He'd poured himself a whisky in the drawing room. As she walked in, she saw him slam the glass down on the chimney-piece, and stand motionless, staring into the empty fireplace, his back to her, tension in every line of his body.

'Marco...? We have to talk... You can't just make a statement like that and walk out on me...!'

He turned to look at her. It was dimly lit in the drawing room—only one table lamp was switched on—but she registered with shock that there were tears on his face.

'Oh... Marco...' Her own throat choked; she could hardly speak.

'Go back to the terrace.' He raked a hand over his eyes, snatched a furious, shuddering breath. She reached to touch his shoulder and felt a fierce reaction go through him; the powerful muscles locked under her fingers as he shrugged her away.

'No...I can't, we have to talk this through,' she whispered unsteadily. She clenched her hands helplessly at her sides, staring at him, willing him to listen.

'Not now, Polly.' He met her anguished gaze bleakly. 'We'll talk later. Right now, I need some space...'

'It's been hard for me too, you know,' she felt entitled to point out. 'Bringing up Ben alone...'

'But you *had* him.' His voice was suddenly deep and fierce. 'I have been denied him. I had a baby son and I never knew him. He could have had two loving parents right from birth, but you denied him that. I'm not sure I can forgive you for that, Polly...'

Suddenly Marco seemed far more Sicilian than English, she thought with a shiver. His words had a dramatic, vengeful ring that no Englishman she knew would ever achieve. She stared at his dark, hard-boned face in the soft light. He wasn't crying any more; the dark eyes looked brilliantly black, shadowed in deep sockets. But the pain he was feeling seemed to transmit itself to her in the silence.

She could hardly bear it. Reaching out her arms, she grasped him by the shoulders, stepped close to wrap her arms round him. She was trembling all over with emotion. Marco caught a ragged breath and stood rigid in her arms. Driven by a need stronger than reason, she reached up to touch her mouth to his; electricity surged between them as their lips touched.

With a thick, muffled curse, he caught hold of her head and kissed her hungrily in return; she parted her lips and he thrust inside and their tongues entwined, heightened by the violence of emotions. His mouth tasted of whisky. A flame flickered, then leaped into a furnace of desire so potent she felt as if her body might fuse with his in the heat.

'Please don't hate me...' she half sobbed against his mouth. 'Please, I couldn't bear that...'

'I don't hate you...' His voice was jagged with pain. 'God help me, I should hate you, but I don't...'

She could hardly breathe. Her breasts were swelling against him, throbbing with desire; her stomach felt hollow with need; her knees were boneless. He raked a hand down her back and pressed her hips against him; she felt the hard outline of his arousal. He might be furious with her. But physically, at least, he still wanted her...

If he'd pushed her to the floor right there and undressed her she'd have made no protest; she'd have welcomed him mindlessly, with an urgency that made her deeply ashamed of her lack of control...

Marco stroked his hands around her ribcage, spanned the smallness of her waist, tracing the contours of her body through the soft material of her dress.

She gave a choked cry as he moved shaking fingers to the buttons, tore the top three open, smoothed the warm flesh inside with a kind of hungry intensity that consumed her with helpless desire. She clung to him, her eyes shut tightly on violent swirls of colour, as his hands pushed away the lace of her bra and his lips grazed a tight nipple. The surge of passion was sharpened by a suppressed fury. It emanated from him so powerfully it was almost visible, like an aura of white-hot rage surrounding his body. She wondered what she'd ignited. For a few stunned seconds she felt the clutch of cold fear mingling with the molten heat in her stomach.

'I've missed you...' she whispered thickly, half-blind with wanting him, the hopelessness of the situation briefly giving way after years of starving for his touch. 'Oh, Marco, you have no idea how much I've missed you...'

'Missed me? Don't lie, Polly,' he groaned roughly, then with a fierce shudder, as if he'd suddenly come to his senses again, he released her and they broke apart abruptly.

Marco's face was in shadow, but his eyes were fixed on Polly;

he was breathing heavily, dragging huge, painful breaths into his lungs; she could see the passionate glitter of his anger.

'I was only ever a phone call or an air flight away!' he added huskily.

No, you weren't. You were Sophy's! Polly thought in anguish. She stared at him mutely.

'You were carrying my child. Didn't it occur to you that I had a right to know? But you didn't tell me. You deliberately avoided me all this time, hiding your pregnancy, hiding my son from me. My God, Polly, how could you do that...?'

'Marco...oh, please...' She couldn't help herself; tears stung her eyes and began to run down her face.

Her fingers numb, her eyes blurred, she tried to fasten the buttons on her dress.

Marco watched her fumbled efforts for a few seconds, then roughly brushed her hands away and did them up himself.

'It's okay, don't cry,' he said, his voice thick and rough with emotion. 'You were right, we do need to talk. Do you want something stronger to drink?'

'No...yes, okay...'

He poured her a whisky and handed the glass to her. His eyes were cooler again, as if the practical action of fetching her the drink had given him time to control his feelings.

'The first thing we need to sort out is how we get Ben out here, as quickly as possible...'

'I'll fly back...' she began uneasily.

'No.' Something in his voice made her swivel her head to stare at him. 'I'm not letting you out of my sight again for the moment,' he said huskily. 'I'll ask Sophy to bring him out.'

'*What?*'

The blood seemed to have left her veins; she was suddenly so cold. He was actually suggesting that *Sophy* bring Ben out to Italy... she could hardly believe his insensitivity...

'It's the obvious solution.' Marco sounded coolly matter-of-fact. 'She's his aunt; I'll check out the precise legal situation first thing in the morning, but I've a feeling that in a case like this all you and I need to do is sign an authorisation at the Consulate in Florence and have it faxed through to the Passport Office in

London. Emergency passports can be issued the same day. Sophy would have to fill in some kind of form...'

'Presumably one of the advantages of being a lawyer,' she commented bitterly, 'is that your head is full of such obscure information?'

'And she'd have to produce his birth certificate, of course. You know where that is, I presume?'

'At home. In the bureau.' She took a sip of the whisky, trying to steady herself. 'But, Marco, I don't want Ben flown out here for us to...to fight over, or something...!'

Marco looked at her, his eyes unreadable.

'I would do nothing to harm our son, Polly, in any way. Ben's welfare is my only concern. But I want him here. And I want you here. I don't trust you to fly back to England and bring him to me. This way, God willing, our son should be reunited with both his parents within the next couple of days...'

'And what then?' Polly demanded flatly. She could hardly believe he was taking charge so...arrogantly. Involving Sophy, even though he must know how intolerable that was going to be....

But guilt was tempering her anger. Marco's fierce response to discovering he was Ben's father was leaving her feeling rather as if she'd been flattened by a steamroller.

'Let's discuss that another time, shall we?' he said coolly. 'Now, I need dinner. And I think, in the circumstances, we'll eat out.'

The next twenty-four hours passed in a haze of tension and misery. The necessary arrangements were made and proved surprisingly easy, just as Marco had predicted. Polly had no idea how he persuaded Sophy to ditch her modelling job and travel out with Ben, but it seemed that in this case what Marco wanted, Marco succeeded in getting. He even knew the right person to pull strings with the airline, and managed to miraculously get two last-minute standby seats from Heathrow to Florence for the following evening.

Throughout it all he behaved like a distant, polite stranger. After that initial loss of control—which she had triggered by practically throwing herself at him, she reflected bitterly—he'd been careful not to touch her. Presumably the thought of being reunited with Sophy at the same time as meeting his son for the first time was giving him quite enough to occupy his mind.

Polly tried to steel herself for the unbearable situation about to manifest itself in her life, but no amount of steeling prepared her for the emotional devastation of finally hearing the car door slam in the courtyard, hearing the voices and footsteps crunching on the sandy-red pebbled path leading round to the house, seeing the group come into view.

Aunt Ruth and Uncle Tino had gone to meet them from the plane—Marco had insisted that the delicate first meeting between himself and his son should take place at home, not at the airport.

Polly ran to the door and watched Ruth and Tino, and Sophy and Ben, approaching Marco's farmhouse. Marco was already there, standing very still. Even though they weren't touching, she could tell that his muscles were rigid with tension. His eyes were fixed on the small figure at Sophy's side.

'*Ciao*, Marco! Hi, there, Pollyanna!' Sophy's cool, high voice travelled easily on the clear evening air.

Marco moved at last, and slowly went to greet them.

Polly stayed where she was, one hand on the doorframe for support. She watched his back view, lean and broad-shouldered, deceptively casual in jeans and a loose shirt, walking towards Ben and Sophy, and found herself transfixed with the horror of it all. The scene was fragmenting into a series of vivid images. As Sophy came closer Polly could see that her stepsister's smile was fixed and false, that the beautiful violet eyes were overbright, feverish, glittering with suppressed resentment, or excitement, or both. She was holding Ben's hand tightly, tugging him along like a captured trophy as she stepped quickly up to Marco and embraced him, kissing him on each cheek, then hugging him tightly. It was a little ritual of possession, for Polly's benefit.

She felt a pain in her stomach, gnawing and heavy. Until this moment she'd begun to doubt her motives in the past. But now she recognised how right she'd been to run from Marco's attempts to see her again after Cambridge. How right she'd been to keep Ben's existence secret...

The small figure at Sophy's side detached itself with a husky shout, and broke into a run.

'Mummy! Mummy! We flew here on an air'plane. Sofa says I can eat real 'talian spaghetti!' Ben's excited voice, with his familiar and slightly unfortunate version of Sophy's name, broke the unreal spell for Polly. With a surge of intense pleasure which clenched her stomach she gave a choked cry of greeting and held out her arms to her son. As he reached her she gathered him to her, lifting him up and ruffling his hair, kissing his soft cheek, laughing as he laughed at her.

Then she turned to look at the others.

Tino, Marco's father, was as tall and dark as his son, and remarkably like him, except for the iron-grey of his hair and deeply etched lines on his face. His expression tonight was wry and wary, an unreadable gleam in his dark blue eyes.

Aunt Ruth was smiling fixedly, a cloud of uncertainty in her eyes as she began a nervous account of traffic and airport parking, covering the tension with meaningless chatter. Throughout this Polly couldn't take her eyes off Marco. He was still standing by Sophy. Sophy had put her arm round him and was rhythmically stroking his shoulder, as if offering silent support in his moment of emotional crisis.

His gaze flicked briefly to Polly, then narrowed again on the small, dark-haired boy in her arms.

'This is Ben,' she supplied unnecessarily. Her throat was so dry, her voice came out on a croak.

Marco's blue gaze was warm and fiercely proud as he smiled at Ben.

'Yes. So I see. Hello, Ben.'

She slowly put Ben down, took his hand in hers, and stared helplessly at Marco.

Sophy seemed to be poised on her toes, staring from one to the other, hardly breathing. She looked, if anything, even more glamorous than normal, in a short scarlet dress with her golden blonde hair pinned up on top of her head, tendrils trailing around her face; a lot of mauve eye make-up accentuated the brilliance of her violet eyes.

Polly pulled herself together with an effort.

'Maybe we could show Ben where he's going to sleep?' she managed lightly. 'It's well past his bedtime...'

'Yes, of course...' Marco looked briefly at a loss. Then, abruptly, he moved away from Sophy and walked over to Ben. He squatted down and gravely inspected Ben's small face. He made a visible effort to relax, and smile at the little boy. 'How about something to eat, then...maybe a bath and a story, Ben? We've put a bed for you right beside your mummy's bed...'

Ben had slotted a thoughtful thumb into his mouth as he assessed Marco. He continued to stare at him with the fearless gaze of the curious toddler. Polly watched them both, her heart thumping very painfully. She'd always known how alike they were. She might not have seen Marco for four years, but she hadn't even needed photographs to recall his hard, striking features in every detail.

But seeing the two of them now, abruptly face to face, was an agonising revelation. The lonely, secretive years kaleidoscoped in her brain. Ben was Marco's double. Her feelings underwent another abrupt, bewildered reversal. Regardless of pride, regardless of Sophy, how had she dared keep them apart all this time?

Ben, lean and olive-skinned, in his favourite jeans and sweatshirt, with minuscule trainers on his feet, looked so tiny, so vulnerable beside Marco's full-grown male strength. She felt tears prick the backs of her eyelids, and blinked rapidly.

'Who's this man, Mummy?' Ben said finally, his voice slightly muffled round his thumb.

'Marco Daretta.' Before she could find her voice Marco had introduced himself. He held out his hand, took Ben's free hand and shook it formally. 'I think we spoke on the telephone the other day, didn't we?'

Ben stared for a few moments longer, then slowly nodded. He removed his thumb.

'Mummy's cousin Marco.' He pronounced this with evident satisfaction. He'd found a reassuring pigeonhole in his limited world, and slotted Marco into it.

'That's right. Now then...' Rising to his feet, Marco swept a blank glance over them all, and addressed his mother in a low, controlled voice. 'Mother, would you mind showing Sophy her room? And I'll take Ben upstairs and show him his bed...'

'No.' Ben had his stubborn face on. 'I'm staying with my mummy.'

Polly took a quick, shaky breath. She knew that expression. Ben was clearly overtired, over-excited, and now sensed adult dissension. His lower lip had begun to stick out, and to ominously tremble. Any further insecurity and he would be humiliated into bursting into tears, something his pride forbade under all but the most extreme of circumstances.

'Of course you shall stay with Mummy, Ben,' she agreed evenly, picking him up and hugging him close, feeling him wrap his arms tightly around her neck in silent entreaty. 'But...you know you once asked me where your daddy was?'

She felt Ben's small head move against her neck as he nodded slowly. She felt his heart beat slightly faster as she hugged him against her.

'Marco is your daddy, Ben. So let's all go together and find out where you're going to sleep, shall we?'

There was a long silence while Ben turned and looked very hard at Marco.

'If you *are* my daddy,' he said at last, 'why don't you live with my *mummy*?'

The next hour was one of the worst of Polly's life. Superficially, she, Ruth, Tino, Sophy and Marco talked and laughed, and played with Ben, and went through the motions of normality—acting out a convincing scenario of happy family life while beneath the surface a volcano of anger and unspoken questions and accusations simmered close to eruption.

When Ben was finally settled in a bed next to hers, she emerged exhausted onto the landing, to bump straight into Marco. He was leaning against the wall, waiting for her.

She raked a shaky hand through her hair.

'We need to talk,' he said quietly.

'Not here,' she said in a stiff whisper.

'No...' He levered himself off the wall and came to take her upper arm in a gesture that felt both intimate and intimidating.

He led her into a bedroom just along the corridor. 'We won't be interrupted in here...'

'Your room...?'

'Don't worry,' he murmured, 'I've no plans to ravish you tonight, Polly.'

'Even so...' She stood quite still, just inside the room, and stared around her, almost holding her breath. Marco's bedroom was large, square, with walls of bare stone and high, unpainted roof timbers; the ceiling was painted matt white and the floor was covered in coarse, tan-coloured coir matting. The bedcovers gleamed like silk—a cinnamon and white striped fabric, echoed in the curtains. The bed was huge; it looked as if it stood on a raised plinth...somehow it seemed to symbolically dominate the room...

'If we want to talk in private, a walk or something might be preferable.' She flinched away from his fingers. They were digging into her bare upper arm. He suddenly seemed to register how hard he was holding her. He let go, dropped his hand to his side, and stood there staring at her. Almost distractedly, he rubbed a hand over his face.

'Isn't there a chance Ben will wake and want you?'

Polly stared at him, his words sinking in. She was so drained with nervous tension she was hardly thinking straight. But he was quite right. Ben had been bathed and dried, cuddled and kissed, and dressed in his best red and yellow Noddy pyjamas. A Postman Pat story had been read five times, a plate of bread and honey and a glass of orange juice demolished. His bed had been placed next to Polly's, and now the door was ajar, a lamp with a low-watt bulb substituted for a nightlight on the locker by his bed. But there was still a slight chance that he might stir and call for her, and if she wasn't available...

'Yes. It's possible. But if we just go into the gardens...'

'You don't like my bedroom?' His eyes were unreadable, but there was a twist of a smile on his mouth.

'It's not that...' She felt herself going hot. In spite of everything, she longed for him to hold her in his arms. She was ashamed of her lack of pride.

There was a brief silence, and his gaze became lidded as he held hers.

'Okay,' he agreed abruptly, steering her out of the door, 'let's go in the garden...'

Outside it was warm, the darkness scented by flowers. Polly caught a fleeting glimpse of Ruth, Sophy and Tino, sitting together just inside the open French doors, saw in the light of the lamp their faces turn to watch as she and Marco passed.

'He's incredible,' Marco said slowly. They reached the end of the lawn and stopped where paths branched off amongst the flowerbeds. Polly thrust her shaky hands into the pockets of her white jeans, and tried to keep her thoughts on calm, orderly lines.

'Yes, he is...' She swallowed on a dry throat and turned to search Marco's face. 'I'm sorry about the...introduction. It was clumsy of me...'

'It could have been worse. I don't think he'll hold a grudge against my absent fatherhood for too long—not after my last rendition of Postman Pat.'

She met his wry smile and her heart went out to him. Ben's acceptance of him would take time, that was natural, but somehow this fact only served to emphasise her crime in keeping them apart...

'He already likes you,' she said quickly. 'He's normally quite reserved with strangers...'

She saw the glitter in Marco's eyes and bit her lip. This was dreadful. She felt guilty and defensive, and everything she said seemed to make things a hundred times worse...

'How ironic, that I'm a stranger to my own son.'

'Marco, I...'

'At least he's clearly a Daretta,' Marco added flatly, slanting a shadowed look at her in the moonlight. 'He'll be able to see the likeness when he's older. My father says he looks exactly like me at that age.'

'Yes, I'm sure. Not a trace of Hamilton features, I agree. But he's still my son, Marco...'

'Of course. But it's just as well that nature proclaims him so clearly to be *my* son. Otherwise I would still not know, to this very moment, that I was a father.' Marco sounded bitter. 'You had no intention of telling me, did you? Paul would still be playing that role, usurping my rightful position. Am I right?'

She felt her stomach tighten. Marco's anger tonight was quiet, and slow-burning, and somehow all the more alarming. She was opening her mouth to reply, to explain that Paul meant nothing to either herself or to Ben, when Sophy's voice came across the lawn.

'Marco? Polly? Are you there?'

She appeared a few seconds later, looming through the darkness.

'Oh, there you are!' She smiled determinedly at Marco, then glared at Polly, hands on hips. 'Ben's awake; he's had a bad dream, I think. He's asking for you, Poll...'

Polly was running for the house before Sophy had finished talking. When she reached the steps to the terrace, she glanced briefly over her shoulder. Marco and Sophy were nowhere to be seen, lost in the black shadows at the end of the lawn.

She felt a quick, sick lurch of confirmation. So much for Marco's declared commitment to his son, she thought, swallowing a bitter lump in her throat. If Sophy was in the picture, Marco's attention was fully engaged. And so much for his vehement denial of being involved with Sophy. Nothing had changed since that week in Sicily, when he'd seemed mesmerised by her, when he'd watched her every move and laughed at every joke she made, escorted her to every restaurant and bar in the vicinity...

Appalled at the raw power of her jealousy, she pushed the pain to the back of her mind as she dashed into the house and took the stairs two at a time.

Ben was sitting safely cuddled up on Ruth's lap, in the softly lit bedroom. He looked quite happy; there was no trace of tears on his small face and he was sleepy-eyed, thumb in mouth, as Ruth read to him. When he saw Polly his eyes brightened; he lifted his free hand and waggled the fingers briefly in a wave of greeting, concentrating on the story.

'More...?' he tried hopefully, as Ruth finished the book.

Ruth was smiling at him fondly. 'Go back to sleep now, Ben. Say goodnight to Mummy.'

'I'm not sleepy. Mummy, read some more,' he murmured. He held out his arms to Polly. With a wry smile, she lifted him and hugged him close, ruffling his silky black hair. She inhaled the scent of talcum powder on his skin and nuzzled his neck. She wished she didn't feel so much like crying.

'All right, just this once,' she said softly. 'If you promise to close your eyes and try to sleep straight away afterwards.'

He was almost asleep in her arms, she realised, feeling that familiar, still heaviness that heralded sleep. She tucked him back in bed and Ruth crept out as Polly sat down beside him and very quietly began the story again. It was his favourite: an ancient, politically incorrect Noddy book from the nursery bookcase at Hamilton Priory, involving car thefts and goblins and exciting adventures in a dark, dark wood; he'd obviously brought it with him, along with his favourite battered teddy bear. She sent up a cautious prayer of thanks; at least he'd been given some say in the packing, even if it had been sprung as a last-minute surprise. She'd half wondered if he'd ask for his daddy, but he was probably still processing the new information. It was best to leave him to grasp it in his own time, in his own way...

He was asleep before she'd finished the third page.

Polly carefully closed the book, and stared down at her sleeping son. Her heart was bursting with love for him. She loved him so much. He looked indescribably beautiful, and familiar and dear, lying there with his thumb in his mouth, his silky black lashes curving on his olive cheeks, his small teddy bear clutched in his other hand. And yet suddenly he looked remote from her; his uncanny likeness to Marco seemed to set him apart from her. Seeing him here in Italy seemed to emphasise that fact.

She had a vision of a future without him, a premonition of losing him, and cold fingers of dread gripped her stomach, brought a dark cloud of anxiety down on her head. The last few hours had turned her life upside down. She was in a foreign country, with her secret out and Marco simmering with suppressed fury, and Sophy and Marco were alone down there in the gardens...

What were they were doing now? Discussing their next move?

Was Marco going to try to keep Ben for himself and marry Sophy?

A fierce, hot feeling replaced the fear. Until now Ben had depended totally on her. Ben was hers; she'd protect him, fight for him, die for him if necessary... Whatever Marco was planning, she would put Ben's needs first and her own second, but she could never, ever let Ben be taken away from her...

She stood up very slowly, anxious not to disturb Ben, then left the door ajar and made her way slowly, reluctantly, downstairs.

Tino and Ruth were in the large, softly-lit drawing room; Tino was reading a newspaper, gold-rimmed glasses perched on his nose. He lowered it, and smiled slightly as he saw Polly. Ruth laid aside the novel she was reading and patted the sofa beside her.

'Darling, come here. You look shattered. Come and talk to me.'

Polly felt a tug of need; there was nothing she'd like more than to rush to Aunt Ruth, bury her face against that softly rounded shoulder and sob her heart out. But Ruth was Marco's mother. For the time being she'd have to be treated with great caution: a potential ally, but also a potential enemy.

She gave Ruth a strained smile and sat down several inches away from her. She smoothed her fingers nervously over her silk blouse, then folded her arms.

'I'm worried that Marco may be planning to keep Ben here in Italy,' she said shakily. 'I don't think he's going to listen to reason...'

'Darling, he will. Give him time. He's in shock. We...we all are. Where is Marco, anyway?' Ruth glanced around, frowning.

'I don't know. Outside somewhere.' Polly let out a shuddering breath, fighting for control. 'With Sophy, I think.'

'Marco's headstrong. He'll calm down,' Tino commented, over the top of his newspaper. 'He has a son he never knew about, Polly. He didn't need words to tell him the child was his; he took one look and he knew here...' Tino clapped his hand to his heart in a very un-English gesture, his dark eyes glistening with emotion. 'And I have a grandson. This gives me the greatest joy, and the greatest sadness. Because I did not know until now. We Darettas are a close family, Polly. We look after our own, do you understand?'

'Yes, of course she understands, Tino,' Ruth cut in gently. 'Polly's been through enough this last couple of days. She's white as a sheet and she's shaking all over; she doesn't need you lecturing her on family unity...'

'It's all right, Aunt Ruth. I'm quite aware that the Darettas close ranks and protect their own.' Polly stood up stiffly and began to walk out.

Ruth jumped up and caught her arm.

'Sit down, my dear. Tino, get Polly a stiff drink, please...'

'*Si, si, va bene. Mi dispiace.*' Tino leaped to his feet, looking chastened, and went to a drinks table. 'Polly, what would you like?'

'I don't know...' She was gulping back the infuriating need to howl like a baby. It was Ruth's kindness, Tino's bumbling, well-meaning, apologetic concern.

'A strong gin and tonic,' Ruth advised firmly, putting her arm round Polly and giving her a reassuring squeeze.

Tino came across, pressed the drink into her hands.

'Thank you.'

'*Di niente*, Polly. Forgive me, my dear. Relax, things will work out, you'll see. Give Marco time; he'll—'

'He'll what...?' It was Marco's voice, cutting grimly through their conversation from the open French doors to the garden. They all turned round.

Polly nearly dropped her drink. She clenched her hands around it until her knuckles went white. Marco was standing there, gaunt and unsmiling, with one arm tightly round Sophy. Sophy had both her arms wrapped around his body, and was leaning into him as if she couldn't bear to let him go.

'I heard my name mentioned,' Marco prompted. His ghost of a smile didn't come near to reaching his eyes, 'What will I do, Papà? Given time?'

Tino's dark face was every bit as bleak as his son's as he surveyed the scene.

'The right thing,' he said softly. 'Although it seems to me that your life is a little more complicated than I thought, my son...'

Marco had locked eyes with his father for a long moment, with a kind of blank challenge in his gaze, then he seemed to snap back to awareness, glancing swiftly around the silent faces in the room, then down at Sophy, clinging to him weakly.

'Sophy fell and twisted her ankle on the terrace steps,' he explained quickly, his eyes flicking to Polly and narrowing on her tense white face. 'She's finding it hard to walk...'

'Oh, Marco, I told you to get those steps fixed!' Ruth jumped up, eyeing Sophy's brave smile with an uncertain expression in her eyes. 'How bad is it?'

'My ankle really hurts,' Sophy said, in a breathless voice. 'I can't put my foot down at all; it's too painful...'

'If you can manage to come upstairs with me, Sophy dear,' Ruth offered quickly, 'we'll bathe it in cold water. And I'll see if Marco's housekeeper Angelina can find a bandage in the medicine box...'

Sophy made a valiant attempt to hobble to the door with Ruth's support, then gave a cry of pain.

'It's no good. Marco will have to carry me upstairs,' she gasped huskily, stopping and holding out her arms.

Polly felt her jaw clench so tightly she imagined she might never unlock it again.

His expression unreadable, Marco scooped Sophy effortlessly into his arms and disappeared towards the stairs, his mother following.

There was an uneasy silence in the drawing room when they'd gone.

'I think,' Tino said slowly, when the silence had lengthened, 'that I see the problem, *cara.*'

'You do?' Polly could hardly recognise her voice, it sounded bright, brittle, ridiculously defensive. Inside she was dying, drowning in misery, 'You mean you see that your son is crazy about my step-sister?'

Tino looked thoughtful.

'I see that your step-sister is crazy about my son. And that you are jealous of your step-sister. That is not necessarily the same thing...'

'Believe me, Uncle Tino, it all boils down to the same thing,' Polly assured him evenly, blinking back tears, 'I'm not stupid...'

'No you're not,' Marco said from behind her chair. He'd come into the room so quietly, she hadn't heard him.

Twisting round, she glanced at him defiantly.

'Will you stop doing that, Marco?'

'What?'

'Prowling into rooms and...and eavesdropping on other people's conversations.'

'I was hardly prowling,' he pointed out, coming to sit opposite her. 'This is my house. I just walked into my sitting room. And since you claim not to be stupid, Polly, you won't argue when I suggest the obvious solution to our current...dilemma.'

Polly took a long gulp of the gin and tonic. 'Stiff' was an understatement. Galvanised by Ruth's sharp tone, Tino must have put three measures of gin to one measure of tonic. She gasped and coughed. Marco leaned forward and took the glass from her, sniffing it warily, then put it carefully down on the low wooden coffee table between them.

'What's the *obvious* solution, then?' she managed bitingly. 'I conveniently throw myself under a bus, leaving the coast clear for you and Sophy to give Ben a happy home?'

Marco's eyes were hooded as he scanned her white face.

'Fantasising about my relationship with Sophy is a poor method of easing your conscience about Paul. So I'll dismiss that suggestion as the gin talking,' he said, with a mirthless laugh. 'What's *obvious* is that you and I have to get married.'

CHAPTER FIVE

POLLY stared at Marco in silence. Then she jumped up, crashing into the table and knocking her drink over. With a muffled apology she stumbled past it and ran blindly out of the French doors into the warm evening.

She hurried along the terrace towards the courtyard. She was hardly conscious of where she was going. Crossing the courtyard, she reached the dusty track which led out of the farmhouse grounds. It led up the hill into woods and vineyards. She started to run when she heard Marco's voice, the rough surface of the track crunching under her feet. The moon lit up the way ahead quite clearly. If she kept running, surely he'd get the message, realise that the last thing she wanted was his company right now.

'Polly, wait...'

In spite of her pace he caught up with her easily, hardly out of breath, catching her arm, stopping her.

'Leave me alone...' She angrily twisted her arm; he held on.

'Be reasonable. You can't just run off alone, Polly...'

'Ben is safe with Ruth and Tino...' she said coldly. 'He went back to sleep quite happily; he's unlikely to wake again tonight.'

'It wasn't Ben I was worried about. Tuscany may be a relatively safe place, but I wouldn't recommend anywhere for lone females at night.'

'Why would you care?'

'You're being childish.'

'Go away, Marco....' Her anger was making her shake all over.

'I appreciate that you might want some privacy,' he said drily, 'but if you insist on looking for it out in the open countryside at night, you'll have to make do with my company.'

He turned to walk beside her, his hand still trapping her arm. She gave a shuddering sigh. It seemed she had no option. She'd have to walk with him. They walked in silence for a few minutes; above the crunch of their footsteps and her own ragged breathing she could hear only the rustle of small animals in the grass and the shrill sound of crickets.

'I just can't believe,' she managed finally, 'that you expect me to marry you.'

'Don't you think our son deserves two parents who love him? From now on Ben is going to have a conventional upbringing, with both his parents in attendance. The best way to make sure that happens is for us to marry, Polly...'

She gasped with disbelief, rounding on him abruptly. They'd reached the top of the hill, where a massive oak tree marked the beginning of a wood.

'What sort of environment will he grow up in if his father and mother loathe the sight of each other?'

Marco gazed at her for a long moment, his beautiful eyes lidded.

'You loathe the sight of me?' Without warning, he lifted his hands and caught her upper arms, drawing her close. 'That's not the message you were giving out yesterday...'

Polly held her breath; irrespective of her emotional state, his nearness was hot temptation, affecting her physically to such a degree she started to tremble. The tips of her breasts made contact with the breadth of his chest; even through their clothing her reaction to him was swamping her defences.

'This isn't fair, Marco...'

'Isn't it? I got the impression in the drawing room last night that you'd be happy to put our relationship back on a more...intimate level...' He dropped his mouth to hers, to block her protest. With a shudder she involuntarily let her lips part; electric shocks of desire jarred through her veins.

'Well?' he persisted huskily, lifting his head a fraction. 'Did I get the wrong impression?'

She stared at him, heart pounding. She should be retaliating. He was cruel to be using last night's moment of weakness as a weapon against her; she felt embarrassed enough about the way she'd been unable to disguise her feelings.

But Marco held her gaze, and she found herself half mesmerised, drawn into the darkness of those deep-set eyes. He abruptly let go of her, and then he was shrugging off his jacket, bending to spread it on the ground beneath the shadow of the oak tree. When he drew her down to sit beside him she let it happen, as if she were in a trance. He put an arm round her and she found she was holding her breath again, unbearably conscious of the iron-hard muscle of his body next to hers.

'Polly, whatever you say, I think you probably know how I feel about you,' he said softly. '*Cara*, ever since you came out here I haven't been able to stop thinking about making love to you.'

She stared straight ahead, her heart thudding erratically. She tried very hard to sublimate the effect he was having on her by concentrating on the beauty of the Italian night all around them. Through a blur of tears she could see the lights of Marco's farmhouse in the distance, pinpoints of welcoming gold in the dark.

She thought of Sophy down there, happily ensconced in a guest room, with her sprained ankle and that triumphant gleam in her eye. The vision gave her strength. She suddenly knew the lie she needed to use to defend herself...

'Lust is hardly a basis for marriage, Marco. Maybe it's untrue to say I loathe the sight of you...' she confessed huskily. She found herself swallowing a lump in her throat as the rush of emotion rose to choke her. 'But getting...getting sexually aroused by someone is one thing... Do you honestly think we should even contemplate marriage when...when we're neither of us uninvolved and heartfree?'

She bit her lip in anguish as she felt Marco's hard body go tense beside her.

'You're talking about Paul, I presume,' he bit out softly. 'Are you sleeping with him?'

'I don't have to tell you everything. Any more than you have to tell me that you're sleeping with my stepsister...'

He twisted to stare at her, his eyes lidded.

'*Basta!* Enough, Polly! I'm sick of hearing Sophy's name. I'm tired of hearing it linked with mine!'

She stared at his face, bleak and intense in the moonlight, and angrily blinked back tears.

'How am I supposed to convince you that I'm not involved with Sophy?' he ground out hoarsely.

She closed her eyes, feeling a wave of fresh confusion.

'With great difficulty,' she said at last, 'since actions speak louder than words.'

'Whatever actions you're talking about,' he said slowly, 'your stepsister and I are just...friends. There's such a thing as circumstantial evidence, Polly...'

'You'd know all about that, of course, in your line of work. You're also an expert in making a persuasive case for the defence, aren't you?'

She heard the bite of sarcasm in her own voice and hated herself. Wasn't she just blocking him out? Refusing to listen? Her stomach churned in panic. She wanted so much to believe what he was saying. She longed desperately to believe him. But to do so would be to put all her trust in him, and to disregard all the evidence which convinced her he was lying. To risk believing him was too frightening, would make her too vulnerable...

'So you're determined to see me as a liar?' Marco demanded grimly. 'Let's talk about the way you've been deceiving me for the last four years, shall we? If I hadn't seen that photograph, you weren't going to tell me that I had a son. Were you?'

A wave of heat rose and faded in her face. She stared at the ground.

'No...'

'That's what hurts most.' The bitterness in his voice made her catch her breath. He reached out his hand and took her chin with his thumb and forefinger, tilting her face up to his. There was a fierce glitter in his eyes. 'If there was a law which made it a crime to do what you've done to me, you'd be behind bars, Polly.'

There was something chillingly truthful in his soft, furious statement. She twisted her head away and sat there shivering with frustration, gripping her hands around her bent knees.

'I see. You'd ideally like to see me in prison. Failing that, you've decided the next best plan of action is to marry me,' she said slowly. 'How romantic.'

'A boy needs his father, Polly.' His voice was soft, but edged with steel. 'I wouldn't want to separate him from you, obviously, and—'

'But you'd try if necessary?' she cut in unsteadily. She felt tears rise up in her throat, choking her, fierce, angry tears she couldn't hold back any longer. 'Maybe you think with your legal training you'd win? I'd fight you every step of the way, Marco...'

'Polly...' He turned to stare at her, his eyes bleak. He saw the tears, and with a muffled swear-word he wrapped his arms round her and pulled her close. 'Listen to us.' He laughed abruptly. 'Threatening each other with retribution, like sworn enemies. Sweetheart, let's stop fighting and think about Ben...'

'Let go of me...'

'Not until you stop fighting me...'

'Never,' she bit out thickly. 'Don't think for a single minute that I'd let Ben go. I'd never do that, Marco.'

'You won't have to,' he pointed out huskily, staring at her tear-stained face for a long moment before dropping his mouth to gently kiss her lips. 'You're not listening to me. Ben needs to get to know his father, but he needs both of us, Polly. Marry me... Please?'

'No...'

He deepened the kiss; it had the dual effect of stopping the argument and driving her logical sequence of thought into hot, dark oblivion. She held herself stiffly in his embrace for as long as willpower permitted; then it was useless. She was shivering and boneless as his lovemaking became more hungry and more urgent.

'Polly...' His voice was thick with desire; the sound of it, deep and husky and impatient and desperate rolled into one, triggered irresistible memories, feelings which Polly was quite unable to reject. She writhed in an abrupt convulsion of need, wrapping her arms round his neck, arching blindly against him.

'Sweetheart...' Marco's groan sent her temperature soaring. 'Polly, darling, you're so beautiful...I want you so much...'

'Do you?' she whispered raggedly, as he lifted his head and gazed down at her shadowed eyes and swollen lips. 'I wish I could believe you...'

It's Ben he wants, she thought painfully. I'm just the means to get him...

'Believe it...' Marco was kissing her neck, his fingers in her hair, stroking her nape, holding her with such tender passion she felt her own answering desire swamping her resistance completely.

'Oh, Marco...' She whispered his name like a husky caress, and felt the shudder of response in his body as she touched her fingers to his face, raked into his hair and pulled him closer.

'Believe me,' he repeated unsteadily, 'I want you...' He was unbuttoning her blouse, his strong, supple hands pushing inside with shaky insistence. 'You don't know... Hell, sweetheart, you have no idea how much...'

Her blouse was undone, and he smoothed the amber silk away and touched her breasts; she melted inside. Then he was peeling the lace of her bra away, and she felt the cool night air on her bare skin. He used the weight of his body to push her backwards, one iron-hard thigh edging her legs open, and she closed her eyes tightly, desire rising like a floodtide as she felt his eyes darkly roving over her body while he stroked and smoothed the small high mounds until her nipples were rigid. When he bent to suckle each in turn with slow, mounting hunger, Polly caught her breath in a sharp inhalation, then groaned out loud, her body electrified with need for him.

'Marco, I don't...I can't...' She felt incoherent. Her brain wouldn't function; her lips wouldn't form the right shapes to make the words she sought to protect herself.

'Don't worry...it's okay...trust me, sweetheart, this is okay...' The huskiness in his whisper was mesmerising. He was moulding his hands lower, down to the waistband of her jeans, sliding the zipper down and easing the white fabric over her hips, peeling the jeans right off, then hitching a place for himself between her bare thighs, with a possessive male demand as old as time. His seeking fingers cupped the warm feminine mound between her legs, stroking her through the satin of her panties. She gasped, and he plunged his tongue inside her mouth at precisely the moment he slipped a finger beneath the wet satin and found her moist, hot secret with delicate insistence.

Polly was spiralling down and down, into a dark well of desire as fathomless and mysterious as the depths of the ocean. At least this made sense of her weakness four years ago... The thought drifted briefly through her hazy consciousness; when Marco touched her, she lost control. She was no longer able to think clearly. Whether or not he was her stepsister's lover seemed to lose shape and substance, to dissolve into shadowy unimportance...

'Marco...?' Her whispered, unfinished question seemed to hang in the night air.

'Let me in, darling...' The ragged plea was torn from him, hoarse and irresistible. He was pulling her small white satin panties down over her hips, and she gasped and wriggled, clutching his waist, struggling with trembling hands to rip the buttons of his shirt open, to unbuckle the belt of his jeans and unbutton the flies over a bulge so hard the material was stretched to the limit. The blood was thundering in her ears and she gave up, gasping with slightly hysterical laughter as he finished undressing himself with a wrench of impatience and tumbled back on top of her, hot and lean and hard, probing and thrusting into slick, tight, welcoming heat, stifling her cries of passion with his mouth.

It felt like coming home, such a deep, emotional release that she was sobbing hot, wild tears as he drove her to violent climax, then surged and erupted inside her with a muffled shout of triumph.

They collapsed together on the crumpled linen of his jacket. Polly lay like a broken doll; her blood was still drumming fiercely through her veins and she could hear her laboured breathing, feel Marco's hands stroking her hair, caressing her back, determinedly holding her as close as possible.

They lay, wrapped together, for a long time. Polly could hear the thud of his heartbeat vibrating through her own body, feel the overpowering security of being held in his arms. She never wanted the feeling to end...

'Are you on the Pill this time?' he said at last. There was a rough catch of humour in his voice which made her stomach hollow.

'No...'

'Good. I don't want my son growing up an only child.'

Polly lay very still. Marco's teasing arrogance had brought her back to earth with a crash. She could feel her whole body stiffening in mounting outrage. She'd been demented to let this happen; as if she hadn't had enough evidence already, her worst fears had just been confirmed. Marco wasn't, and never had been, emotionally committed to her. He valued her only as the mother of his son, with a kind of possessiveness which took her breath away.

Whereas she, heaven help her, was secretly still so bound up in him she'd give anything for him to care for her in return.

Which gave him so much power to hurt her, she flinched at the prospect.

'Whilst I wouldn't want Ben to be deprived of brothers and sisters,' she choked out with a bitter laugh, 'you could at least try to pretend that your marriage proposal was about more than Ben, and a sibling for Ben, and Ben's security and Ben's environment...'

'Maybe it is,' he said evasively. 'But right now, I don't know, Polly.'

'Oh, what's the point? What's the point of even trying to talk to you...?'

'Quite.' Marco sounded cooler; he shifted away from her slightly. 'You've avoided talking to me for four years. Why break the habit now?'

She sat up abruptly, fumbling for her blouse and jeans, suddenly overwhelmed with humiliation and self-disgust; she'd lost control with him again, just because his slightest touch ignited something she couldn't quench.

She'd never had this problem with any other man, she reflected, pressing her hands to her hot cheeks. In fact, she'd found it quite easy to say no to every other sexual advance that had been made to her. Marco's effect on her was shattering, and the unfairness of the situation hit her like a blow to the stomach. Of all the men to be irresistibly attracted to, it had to be Marco, who'd always shown every sign of loving another woman...

'Polly, darling...'

'Don't call me that.' She'd managed to get dressed, with fingers feeling half-paralysed and refusing to obey her.

'Listen—this is my fault.' Marco stood up, fastening his shirt, pulling on his jeans with swift, measured movements. 'I shouldn't have joked about the Pill. It was in bad taste. I'm sorry.'

She saw the wry gleam of self-mockery in his eyes. For a second she wanted to laugh, make some light retort, break the ice again. Anything to recapture the brief, heady intimacy they'd just shared. But her emotions felt locked inside. Her surrender to Marco, her indulgence of her own needs, now seemed like a sordid physical interlude. As for their relaxed, wonderful day out together, that seemed like a lifetime away instead of just a few short days ago. She turned away, climbing to her feet, and finished fastening her jeans with shaking fingers.

'Come back to the house,' he ordered softly, bending to retrieve his jacket. He shook the dry grass and leaves off it, then put it around her shoulders. He stroked his hands slowly down her arms, searching her face with a slight frown of concern. 'We need to eat; hopefully Angelina is fixing something for us all.'

'I don't want to eat anything,' she managed huskily, shrugging off his hands, stiffly turning to regain the track which led back down the hill. 'Least of all in a big family group. I'm tired; I'll just go to bed...'

'You need to eat something. You're too thin.'

'Do you imagine you're going to try to fatten me up, ready for more breeding?'

His glance was wary as they walked back.

'Post-coital conversation seems to be a problem when you and I get together, Polly.'

'Maybe that's because we're not meant to...to *get together*.'

He was silent for a few paces.

'If that were true, then why do we enjoy it so much?'

Her cheeks had begun to burn again.

'I don't...' she started lamely.

'Liar.' His soft accusation was totally justified, she knew. 'I've only made love to you twice, Polly. And both times you were as wild for me as I was for you.'

'Stop boasting!'

'I'm not boasting. It was mutual.' They'd nearly reached the drive to the farmhouse. He stopped and caught her arm, spinning her round to face him. 'Believe it or not, I'm not in the habit of seducing virgins without contraceptive protection, nor do I regularly pounce on females *al fresco* and make love to them on my jacket.' His wide mouth twitched slightly as he stared down at her. 'So if nothing else, we're talking about serious sexual attraction here... Polly, for Ben's sake at least, don't run out on me tonight. We need to talk things through.'

She felt sick with her longing to trust him. Every atom in her body willed her to do so. Instead, she heard her pride saying coldly, 'Yesterday you said you weren't sure you could ever forgive me for what I'd done. And a little while ago you talked about seeing me behind bars! So excuse me if I find this...this change of tactics a bit suspect?'

She had the brief victory of seeing his eyes flicker with confusion.

'I was angry,' he said finally. There was an edge to his voice. She'd just reminded him of how angry he'd been, she reflected, with a stab of black humour. 'I said some wild things. You can hardly blame me, Polly.'

'Can't I? You seem to think you're totally in the right here, Marco! What about you and Sophy?' She let the words pour out unchecked, hurt and bitter. 'You and my stepsister have been an item for years; I wasn't going to break up your relationship by announcing I was having your baby! So don't try and make me feel like the only one to blame. And please don't keep insulting me by trying to tell me there's nothing going on between you two. I'm not blind. I'm not stupid. Even your father could see that there's something going on...'

'Polly, in hell's name, she'd just twisted her ankle...' The low growl of anger in his voice didn't stop her. She ignored the hardening of his eyes, the flash of fury.

'There was no need for her to be wrapped quite so tightly around you, if that's all it was! Everything you do just proves it. She was automatically the person you chose to accompany Ben out to Italy...'

'She was the obvious choice!'

'Janie would have brought him, if we'd asked her. But naturally you wanted Sophy here! You jump to attention whenever you catch sight of her. She practically devours you with her eyes. You didn't even bother coming in to see if Ben was okay earlier; you stayed in the garden together...'

'What the hell do you think we were doing?'

She gave him a scathing glare, suppressing her shudder of anguish. 'I'd rather not know what you were doing, exactly!'

'We were talking.' Marco sounded grimly furious.

'Whatever you say,' she shot back sarcastically. 'Excuse me if I don't believe you...'

'You say you love Ben.' There was a hint of rough desperation in Marco's voice. 'Even if you see me as a liar, as a man without principles who would make love to your stepsister at the same time as I'd make love to you, you must see that my son needs his father...'

'He's *my* son!'

'He is our son.'

They stared at each other for a long moment. Polly took in the shadowed eyes, the gauntness of Marco's expression; her heart gave a painful jolt in her chest.

'Yes. Yes, he is.'

Marco gazed at her in tense silence for a few more moments. Then he swung round with a wry, courteous gesture, indicating the path leading back to the house.

'Shall we go in, Polly?'

She followed him, clutching his jacket around her. She wished she didn't feel so much like bursting into tears again.

Dinner was a tense affair. Sophy, declaring her ankle to be much better since the doctor had been summoned from the nearby village to bandage it professionally, had managed to hobble down to join them. She'd taken her hair down, and it glowed like golden silk in a riot of curls down her back. She'd also found time to reapply her make-up, and her long violet eyes were stunningly ringed with charcoal, her full pouting mouth a luscious shade of strawberry-pink. She'd changed into a little designer-label black dress, which plunged low at the front and finished a considerable way above her knees.

Next to her, Polly felt plain, boring—a pale shadow in comparison.

She despised herself for letting her self-confidence slip so easily. It wasn't that she'd made no effort. She'd gone to her room, checked on a peacefully sleeping Ben before dinner, then she'd showered, burningly conscious of the sticky, intimate aftermath of their lovemaking, of faint tenderness around her buttocks and spine where she'd allowed herself to be crushed against the hardness of the earth while writhing in uninhibited ecstasy, oblivious to everything but Marco...

She'd washed her hot face, brushed her hair, changed into her linen dress, found some fresh underwear and put on some more peach-pink lipstick and a touch of blusher. Her own hair hung in a pale barley curtain down her back, and at least she didn't look as deathly white as she had earlier. But feeling eclipsed by Sophy in Marco's presence was a habit acquired over the years. It was hard to break.

Angelina and Ruth had cooked the dish Marco had once promised to cook himself, for just the two of them, before this nightmare had begun. It was delicious: a mouthwatering blend of locally raised beef with wild mushrooms and red wine, served with diced pan-fried potatoes and some wonderfully fresh carrots and broccoli. It was so good that, in spite of everything, Polly found her appetite returning.

Seeing her eating, Tino approvingly poured her an enormous glass of red wine, and urged her to a second helping. Ruth pressed her earnestly to more vegetables and sauce. Polly began to feel like an invalid, recovering from a long illness.

'A good meal, good wine, and a good night's sleep,' Tino pronounced jovially, glancing round the table as if challenging anyone to disagree. 'The cure for most things, in my opinion.'

Marco gave a thin smile at the assembled guests around his table.

'If only life were that simple,' he murmured flatly.

'Do I gather *congratulations* are in order, Pollyanna?' Sophy's sarcastically phrased question, delivered into the silence which followed Marco's words, made everyone stop eating and stare from Polly to Sophy and back again.

They were eating at a long, white-clothed table in the dining room, with the doors open onto the terrace and the dark gardens beyond. Polly stared fixedly at a large moth which had fluttered in and was singeing its wings on one of the glass-shaded candles.

'Not now, Sophy...' Marco murmured warningly.

'Oh, dear, have I spoken out of turn?' Sophy persisted, drinking her wine slowly and scanning the faces around the table.

'Leave it, Sophy,' Marco said in a hard voice.

'But Tino said that you'd asked Polly to marry you. In the drawing room. A couple of hours ago...' Sophy shrugged, pushing her knife and fork together on an empty plate. 'Now that the secret's out. About Ben, I mean.'

'I hate to disillusion you in your simplistic view of things, Sophy,' Polly said quietly. She was hanging onto her temper and her dignity with a grave struggle. 'But there's a little more to it. Neither Marco nor I are...are free to commit ourselves to such a marriage...'

'Well, how true! But of course Ben's the one you'll both be thinking about now, isn't he?' Sophy barged on, regardless. 'You'll be making the ultimate sacrifice for him. Mind you, couples I've known who've married for the sake of a child have always come unstuck...'

Polly stared at her stepsister in furious disbelief. The wide-eyed innocence in Sophy's eyes was belied by the vindictive smile on her mouth. Ruth was concentrating carefully on her meal. Tino was drinking his wine slowly, staring into its depths as if it held something of riveting interest.

'Polly and I have a lot to talk about,' Marco said softly. 'We'll work something out. Between ourselves.'

'Well, I expect you've got Dad's blessing,' Sophy continued sweetly, ignoring the pointed message in Marco's tone. 'He was only saying the other day it would be nice if the new generation could heal the family feud by marriage. Still, marrying someone you don't love is a high price to pay, don't you agree?'

'For God's sake, Sophy,' Marco erupted, his dark face taut with annoyance, 'will you stop *bloody* well stirring?'

'Stirring?' Sophy was all innocence. 'Charming. Just trying to offer practical help and advice...'

Marco slowly reached across and folded his hand around Polly's; his touch sent a thousand volts through her nervous system. She tried to withdraw her hand. Marco tightened his fingers, trapping her. She was acutely aware that if Marco's hand were not pinning her down next to him, she'd be running upstairs. Instead, it was Marco who stood up, pushing his chair back with controlled violence, and pulled Polly to her feet.

'Excuse us, would you?' He flicked a cold glance around the table, then looked at Tino and added firmly, 'It's too late tonight, but would you mind taking Sophy back to your place in the morning? Polly and I need some time alone.'

'*Si, si. Va bene...*'

'Marco, that's not very friendly...' Sophy's creamy complexion showed two hot circles of colour in each cheek.

'Maybe I don't have time to be very friendly right now,' he snapped softly.

'Yes, well, I can appreciate you've got other things on your mind, darling. But after all the trouble I've gone to for you...'

Polly had had enough. She tried to tug her hand out of Marco's, but he had her in an iron grip, and he tightened it to keep her at his side.

'Don't send Sophy away on my account,' she said icily. 'All I need is my return flight brought forward, and Ben and I will be out of here on the first plane to Heathrow...'

Ruth had risen and begun to clear the dishes, her round face pink with distress. Tino followed suit.

Only Sophy sat and watched the battle, her violet eyes glittering with malice.

'Now *that* would be a wise decision,' she said softly.

'*Basta.*' Marco's growl was ominous. 'Come on, Polly...'

She found herself frogmarched out of the dining room, across the hall and into the study. Marco pushed her down in one of the chairs by the garden door and sat down opposite, glaring at her.

'Are you going to let her wind you up?' he demanded huskily, searching her white face. His long, glittering eyes looked coal-black in the candlelight. 'That's all she's trying to do, Polly. Hell, I knew you two didn't get along, but I had no idea it was this bad...'

She hardly heard his words. All she could concentrate on was trying to control the bitter agitation inside. She slowly rubbed her fingers, where he'd crushed them.

'You knew we didn't get on? How? From one of your many intimate little chats with my stepsister?'

'Don't use that against me. You're the one who's been avoiding contact with me all these years.'

'For reasons that should be getting clearer and clearer to you by the minute! For pity's sake, Marco, Sophy's right! You don't love me, and...and I don't love you! It's quite obvious that it's Sophy you should be marrying...'

'There's no question of my marrying Sophy,' Marco retorted huskily. 'If I'd wanted to marry Sophy, I'd have done it years ago. It's you I want, Polly.'

'Ben, you mean. It's Ben you want. Be *honest*...!'

'Both of you,' Marco told her softly, his gaze intent. 'You and Ben. I want both of you...'

She stared at him, too choked to speak. The scene at the dinner table had been too humiliating. She could hardly bear to hear him justifying his motives, trying to convince her...

'Listen to me, Polly. Maybe you don't love me, but we'll make the best of the mess we're in. We'll make a family for Ben. You and I. If we don't, it's Ben who'll suffer...' His husky voice held an urgency, a powerful persuasiveness she found hard to dismiss. 'He'll be deprived of stability; he'll grow up wondering why his father didn't care enough; he'll suffer all the disadvantages of a child of a one-parent family, a boy without his father.' He leaned forward, his elbows on his knees, his dark eyes holding hers with a blaze of conviction that almost dazzled her. 'That's not what I want for my son. Is that what *you* want?'

CHAPTER SIX

'You know it isn't!' she managed at last, gathering her tattered defences. 'But if you can't see my reasons for keeping Ben to myself, and if you can't see that our marriage would be a sham that would harm Ben more than the present situation, then you're even more pigheaded and arrogant than I thought...'

Polly ground to an abrupt halt, staring at Marco. With a horrified flash of insight she recognised what she was doing. In rejecting Marco's proposal of marriage, she wasn't protecting Ben's interests. She was trying to protect herself.

Because Marco would make a brilliant father for Ben. If she'd ever really had any doubts about that, all she needed to do was recall his fierce emotion at seeing Ben for the first time, think of the easy, natural way he'd begun to gain the little boy's trust, helping with the bath, reading him stories in bed. He was wonderful with children. She recalled his gentleness and patience and humour with his little three-year-old niece, Rosa, during that trip to Sicily.

And Ben, being so forward and highly intelligent, was just at the age when he'd been starting to ask questions, to demand answers about who and where his daddy was. Now that he'd found him, he'd never forgive her for depriving him of his daddy again...

She was being selfish. She was just terrified of getting hurt again, she acknowledged miserably. It was she, not Ben, at risk of being harmed. Because she cared too deeply about Marco, and she knew he didn't, couldn't, return the strength of the emotion...

'I wondered how long it would take before we got to this point,' Marco was saying cynically.

'What point?'

'Where we're throwing insults at each other.' He stood up, went across to a drinks cabinet and poured two measures of brandy into large crystal balloon glasses. He came back and handed one to her. His gaze was cool as he met her eyes.

'How did you expect me to react?' she defended herself huskily. 'Did you honestly think your...poor effort at a marriage proposal would make me *happy*?'

'Calm down. You're not being offered such a bad deal.' He went to stand with his back to her by the open window; she glared furiously at the breadth of smooth, muscled back tapering to strong, lean hips. 'You're right about one thing,' he added drily. 'I'm not "uninvolved and heartfree", as you put it. Quite the opposite. And maybe you're not, either. But a lot of women would see this situation as to their ultimate advantage and make the best of it. You won't starve or toil alone to bring up Ben. You won't go short of money, food, clothes—all life's necessities. As for sex...' He paused, took a sip of his brandy, then glanced back at her over his shoulder. His eyes had narrowed to a taunting glitter. 'We can come to some arrangement there, I have no doubt.'

She felt unbearably bereft. He'd just admitted that he was involved elsewhere. That he loved Sophy but felt compelled to do the right thing for Ben's sake. She'd known this was true, but hearing him put it into words was like a sick pain enveloping her heart.

'Forget the last part, anyway,' she said bitterly. 'This evening was a one-off.'

'For old times' sake?'

'If you like.'

Marco's shrug was eloquent.

'I can't see us married and living celibate lives. But there again, maybe you prefer to see yourself in the role of sacrificial lamb. You'll profess to hate every minute of it but dutifully lie back and think of England?'

She was so angry, she was finding it hard to find words. The prospect of being married to Marco was something she hardly dared contemplate, because it aroused too many confusing, conflicting emotions—the strongest being an idiotic yearning, against all common sense, to belong with him, to feel secure in her secret passion for him, to build the idyllic kind of family circle she'd dreamed about for herself and Ben...

'Do you really think,' she managed, 'that if we were married I'd sleep with you, knowing you were having an affair with my stepsister at the same time...?'

'*Basta*, Polly. Enough!' He swung round to face her again, his brandy swirling perilously near to spilling.

The fury in his face made her stiffen involuntarily; his eyes were black with emotion and the lines which ran from his nose to the outer corners of his mouth had deepened to a ferocious scowl. 'Your opinion of me couldn't get any lower; that's clear enough. Don't expect me to bother denying anything any longer. There's no point defending myself to someone who will not hear.'

She put down her brandy with a clatter and clenched her trembling hands into tight fists at her sides.

'How convenient! Never apologise, never explain. Is that your motto from now on?'

He expelled a long, harsh breath.

'If I had anything to apologise for,' he said, 'I would do so.'

They were staring at each other in bitter silence when the telephone rang. Marco went to pick it up. He spoke in Italian, then briefly in English, then held out the receiver.

'For you. Jane Chartwell.'

Jumping up, Polly took the receiver with an unsteady hand. Janie had been impressively calm about the surprise arrangements for Ben, and Polly felt a surge of relief at the thought of speaking to her again. Janie's humorous view of life was one of the things Polly liked so much about her...

'Janie?'

'Polly, darling! Is everything all right? Did Ben arrive safely?'

'Everything is fine...' Polly looked pointedly at Marco, who lifted an eyebrow then prowled out of the room, closing the door rather loudly behind him.

'Poll? Are you there?'

Polly breathed out. 'Yes, I'm here. Sorry—just waiting for some privacy. Oh, Janie, I'm so glad to hear your voice!' She had to take a deep breath again to control the stupid desire to burst into tears.

'I thought I'd give you a ring to see how things were going. You sound a bit shaky. Are you sure you're okay, darling?'

'No, not really.'

'Do you want to talk about it?'

Polly sighed shudderingly. She sat on the edge of the desk and stared at the sky through the window: a black rectangle full of so many stars it could have been an artist's impression. Marco's study was softly lit now, with yellow-shaded table lamps. The room had a comforting, homely feel, despite her agitation.

'Marco's insisting that I marry him.'

There was a silence.

'And...? He's Ben's father, right? So you're considering it?'

'No... I don't know... I can't marry him, Janie! He's...' Polly swallowed, cleared her throat, which was suddenly annoyingly choked. 'Oh, God, I'm sorry. I can't talk about it...'

'You can't leave me hanging in mid-air like this!' Janie exclaimed, horrified. 'He's what? A sadist? A multiple killer? A gangster?'

'Stop it.' Polly had to laugh, despite her strong desire to cry. 'Please, Janie. He's not any of those things. I just can't marry him, that's all...'

'I'm not putting this telephone down until you tell me what's going on!'

Polly lifted her eyes to the ceiling for a long, calming moment.

'He and Sophy have been having a relationship for years. Which is why I couldn't tell him about Ben. He's now insisting we marry to give Ben a stable family. But there's obviously something still going on between them...'

Janie drew in a long breath.

'Polly, darling...' Her friend sounded deeply shocked. 'I'm so sorry. I shouldn't have been joking about it...'

'That's probably the only way to handle it,' Polly said bleakly, 'as a joke. If it wasn't for Ben being so thrilled to discover his father, and Marco's entitlement to get to know him, I'd be laughing hysterically myself at this proposal.'

'What are you going to do?'

'I don't know! What I want to do and what I ought to do are two different things...' Polly gripped the receiver. 'All these years I've convinced myself I was doing the right thing—keeping Ben from Marco, keeping the whole thing a secret—but now...'

'Now you're seeing it from Ben's point of view, and he wants his father?'

'Yes...and Marco's wonderful with him.'

'Darling, do you want me to come out there?'

'Heavens, no! This place is crowded enough already! Marco's parents are here, and Sophy, of course...'

'Stirring?' The wry note in Janie's voice made Polly smile slightly.

'Of course...although this must be very difficult for her, Janie...'

'Marco has rights too, Poll. As Ben's father. Don't forget that.'

Polly's face was burning.

'I know... I just object to being bullied, that's all...'

'Give things time to calm down,' Janie advised. 'Don't make any hasty decisions. Darling, I've got to go. My dear husband has just come in and he's demanding the phone for some medical emergency. Who'd be a GP's wife? Ring me later, okay?'

'Yes, I will. Thanks, Janie. I feel better just hearing your voice...'

'Take care, love...'

Polly cradled the phone and stood staring at it for a long time. When the door opened behind her, she jumped.

'Finished?' Marco was expressionless.

'As you see. Were you listening behind the door?'

'Naturally.' He shot her a glacial look. 'That's the kind of behaviour you'd expect from me, isn't it?'

'I wouldn't put anything past you!'

Marco cursed under his breath. For a moment he looked as if he were about to hit her. Then he abruptly took hold of her arms, pulled her against him. She stood rigid as he embraced her, crushing her against his chest.

'Come on,' he said tautly, 'you need to get to bed.'

As she jerked her head up, he met her angry look with a grimace.

'Not with me,' he assured her bleakly. 'You look shattered. A warm bath and a good night's sleep is what you need.'

She found herself being shepherded, gently but firmly, up the stairs to her room. The dim nightlight they'd left for Ben gave her enough light to see her way quietly in; she went to shut the door on Marco, but he held onto her arm.

'Do you have everything you need?' he asked quietly. 'Would some hot chocolate help you sleep?'

'I have all I need. Thanks. Goodnight.'

He slowly let go of her arm. She stared at him in silence for a few seconds, then began to close the door determinedly in his face.

'Wait...' He held onto the door, forcing his way inside.

'Marco, for the love of God...!' she whispered furiously.

'I just want to look at Ben.'

She stood back, quaking inwardly as he went to stand over the sleeping child. She followed his intense gaze.

Ben lay on one side, his right hand loosely resting on the pillow near his open mouth, his favourite sucking thumb never far from position. Long, silky black lashes smudged the olive curve of his face. His breathing was slow and even.

Marco stared with such fixed concentration she could almost hear what he was thinking. His son. His own flesh. His mirror image. Her hands were trembling. There was a tight, constricting pain around her heart.

'He's amazing,' he whispered hoarsely.

'Yes. I know.'

Marco lifted his eyes to hers; she saw the brilliance in his gaze and had to grit her teeth to hide her own emotion.

'I have to make up for lost time,' he said softly, rapidly. 'You see that, don't you? Don't shut me out, Polly...'

Their eyes locked, shadowy blue-black with grey-blue. She felt transfixed, as if she'd been connected to an invisible electric current. When Marco stepped closer and put his arms round her she couldn't find the willpower to fight her own instincts. It was like an irresistible force, as if her soul took over, reaching out for him even when her brain and her heart pulled back. She found herself involuntarily clutching her arms round him in return, and she felt the fierce shudder of his response. Her eyes closed as he shakily sought her mouth with his. He tasted of brandy, and the way he kissed her was like an infusion of pure alcohol into her system, drugging and exhilarating.

His hands smoothed possessively down her back, moulding them together so tightly she could feel the wall of his chest, the taut plane of his abdomen, the growing hardness in his groin. She gasped, her pulses hammering, her bones melting in the familiar conflagration between them. She wanted to stay here in his arms for ever. She longed for this ridiculous limbo of joy to go on and on.

'We can make this work,' he said, on a ragged outbreath. 'We have to; this is too important to me. I want to marry you, Polly. I'm not involved with Sophy. Will you just believe that? I have never loved Sophy...'

'Oh...but you said...' Her whisper broke, but her heart was abruptly bursting with optimism. What had he said, exactly? That he wasn't uninvolved and heartfree. Maybe that meant... She hardly dared to believe it, but her heart gave a small leap of hope; for a moment she found herself believing that he felt involved with *her*, that he did love *her*, that it could all be sorted out, that they could be happy...

'I'd better let you go to bed.' He groaned softly. 'If I stay any longer I won't be responsible for what happens...'

She gulped back the urge to beg him to stay, to just lie with her and hold her in his arms. Marco was releasing her, slowly, his face dark with desire.

'We might wake Ben,' she whispered, as if to convince herself as much as Marco.

'You need to sleep,' he told her unevenly, bending to kiss her bruised lips again, his gaze lingering where his mouth had touched. 'I'll see you in the morning. We'll talk then...'

He finally dragged his attention back to Ben. He gazed at his sleeping son for a few seconds longer, then turned and went out, closing the door quietly behind him.

Polly slept very badly. She felt hot and restless, confused by the conflict inside her, tossing and turning, unbearably agitated and aching with need. Maybe, by some miracle, Marco did love her? Or, more likely, he didn't actually love her but he desired her, and he wanted to make their relationship work. Even if it was only for Ben's sake, it was a start.

Because she loved him. She admitted it now, to herself, in the darkness of her room. She loved Marco. Deeply, totally, no matter what he'd done or whether he'd deceived her. She'd had a crush on him at thirteen and then she'd fallen in love with him in Sicily, and she'd let him make love to her in Cambridge not just because she'd been half-dazed and confused by that drug, but because she loved him and she'd never stopped loving him...

And this love she felt for him, she reflected, tossing and turning in bed as the feelings unravelled inside her, this secret she'd guarded all these years, was so deep and consuming it could be enough for two...couldn't it? She hugged her revelation to herself as she lay in bed. Marco wanted Ben, loved Ben, and she loved Marco so much it made her ache inside...

Some marriages must have succeeded on shakier foundations than these....

As the hours dragged on her thoughts grew more fevered and irrational. After she finally dozed off, she woke twice, because Ben was murmuring in his sleep, but he didn't wake.

The third time she woke it was a soft tapping noise out on the landing that disturbed her. Turning over exhaustedly, she heard it again. She sat up, wondering briefly if it was someone at her door. Then she realised that someone was knocking on a bedroom door along the landing. And the voice she could hear was Sophy's voice, saying Marco's name. Like a statue, she listened to a door opening, a murmur of voices. On trembling legs, her heart thudding against her ribs, she slid out of bed and opened her door slightly.

She was just in time to see Sophy disappearing into Marco's room. Marco's door closed softly behind her.

Polly shut her own door silently. Like a sleepwalker, she made her way slowly to the bathroom. Shaking uncontrollably now, she took off her nightdress and got into the shower, turned on the tap and stood under the stream of soothing warm water. Only then did she let the silent sobs rack her body. Once she'd started, she couldn't stop. 'Have a good cry,' she could remember her mother saying to her. 'Let it all out. You'll feel better afterwards.' But the vision of Marco and Sophy, together in Marco's bedroom, was too painful to erase with tears.

She cried fiercely, bitterly, until her chest ached, her eyes were swollen and her head throbbed. When she finally staggered out, with birds singing outside and pale dawn creeping through the shutters, she collapsed into bed and fell into a deep, exhausted sleep.

She dreamed vividly, about Marco and Ben. They were playing together on a wide, deserted beach. Marco was kicking a ball, very gently, towards Ben, and Ben was bounding after it and swinging one small foot to kick it back and missing. When he'd missed it on numerous occasions he got upset; he sat down on the sand and started crying. He was calling for her, sobbing, 'I want my mummy,' and then he changed it to, 'I want my daddy.' The words rang out over and over again, like a mantra, then Marco was scooping Ben into his arms and Ben stopped crying, hugging him, laughing...

'Do you want to say "Hello, Daddy" in Italian?'

'Yes.'

'*Ciao, Papà.*'

'Chow, Pappa.'

'*Si, va bene. Ciao, Papà. Molto bene!*' Father and son stared at each other and exchanged identical crooked smiles. Then Marco turned and began to walk away down the beach, with Ben in his arms, and Ben clung to him happily, his arms round Marco's neck. She watched, unable to move or follow, until they were so far away they were a speck in the distance...

'*Molto benny?* What's that?'

'Very good. Your Italian is very good.'

Polly opened her eyes. The voices in her dream were real. The conversation was taking place right here in her bedroom. Marco was sitting on the floor beside Ben's bed, his black hair still damp from a shower, wearing a dark blue checked shirt and jeans. Ben was sitting up in bed, still in his pyjamas.

'Mummy's awake!' he pointed out, pleased. He jumped out of bed and climbed onto hers, sitting on her as she lay huddled beneath the duvet and bouncing up and down excitedly, 'Mummy, Daddy's here. He's going to stay with us always now...'

'Good morning.' Marco's tone was bland. 'Did you sleep well?'

Polly cautiously extracted one arm from the covers and scraped a hand through her hair, which was flopping untidily over her eyes. She swallowed on an annoyingly dry throat. Caught by surprise, she could only manage a sleepy glare.

'What are you doing in here?' she demanded softly.

'That's not very friendly. I brought you a cup of tea.' He nodded to the small locker beside her bed. A blue porcelain mug steamed enticingly. 'Milk, no sugar. Is that right?'

'Yes. Thank you...'

'Daddy brought me some chocolate milk.' Ben pointed to a bright red glass, now almost empty. 'He's going to teach me to swim. Drink your tea, Mummy.'

'If you stop bouncing around, I will,' she said, catching him and kissing his dark, flushed little face. Sitting up, she remembered too late that she hadn't put her nightdress back on after her crying session in the shower. She could picture it, still lying on the bathroom floor in a heap. She snatched the duvet to cover her breasts, but not before Marco had seen that she was naked.

She avoided his eyes.

'Ben, will you go to the bathroom and get my nightdress?'

Ben peered at her solemnly.

'Aren't you wearing it?'

'No...'

'Why not? You always wear your nightdress...'

'Ben...' Her son's dark blue eyes were round with innocence, but she could feel herself growing pinker and pinker.

'Maybe Mummy got hot in the night?' Marco suggested. He'd straightened up and was strolling towards the bathroom. There was a smile twitching at his mouth. He emerged with the short, sleeveless cream shift in his hand and waved it in the air. 'Is this it?'

'Yes.' She gritted her teeth. 'If you could pass it to me, please...'

'It's quite a warm morning. Are you sure you need it?'

She narrowed her eyes in mounting frustration.

'Marco, just give it to me, please...!'

'Mummy's got no clothes on,' Ben interjected seriously. He grabbed the top of the duvet and investigated to satisfy himself that this was true. 'She walks around with no clothes on at home.'

'People do...' Marco confirmed, deadpan. He came closer to the bed, with the nightdress dangling irritatingly out of reach. His eyes focused unrelentingly on the slim expanse of bare shoulders and the soft swell of her breasts as she hugged the duvet around her. 'I'm sure your Mummy looks very nice with no clothes on.'

'Louisa says her daddy and mummy wear no clothes all the time...'

Louisa was a year older than Ben, an equally precocious little friend from the Mother and Toddler Group in their village in Devon.

'She says they never wear anything at all in the bedroom...'

'Quite normal, as I understand it.' Marco nodded sagely, sitting on the edge of Polly's bed and watching the heat colouring her face with narrowed eyes. 'Mummies and daddies have a habit of doing that.'

'Marco, I really would like my nightdress, thank you.' The urge to hit him was growing stronger. She had never felt so vulnerable, nor so utterly wretched in spirit. Naked under the duvet—trapped—while he played unforgivable games after spending last night in Sophy's arms...

'Sorry.' He handed it to her with a sudden grin. 'It must be hobnobbing with my small son. I'm behaving like a schoolboy.'

'Are you? "Schoolboy" isn't the term I'd generally use to describe your behaviour.'

'No?' Marco's eyes had darkened, narrowing to speculative slits.

'The connotations are too innocent.' She looked at him coldly.

'I take it you didn't sleep well?' he murmured, searching her set face.

'What makes you say that?'

'Your bad mood?' he suggested drily. 'Or do you make a habit of going to bed in one mood and waking up in a completely different one?'

'Don't we all? Maybe you could get out of my room now? I need to shower and dress.'

'You don't think now is the time for a facts of life lesson for Ben?'

'No, I do not!'

'Okay, I'm going. See you later.'

'See you later,' echoed Ben, a wistful expression on his face as he watched Marco saunter to the door.

'Don't forget the swimming,' Marco said over his shoulder.

Polly watched Ben's face light up.

'Of course I won't,' he said importantly. 'Mummy, what's the fax of life?'

'I want to know what it was like.'

Marco's quiet statement made Polly turn her head in slow enquiry. They were sitting in the warm sun at the edge of the swimming pool in its secluded position down a long, dusty track flanked by vineyards and rolling cornfields. Marco had insisted that they go *en famille*, taking all the necessary ingredients for a relaxed picnic. A small summerhouse contained striped cushions for the wooden sun-loungers at the gravelled poolside, and a rust-red parasol for the wooden table. Crumbling stone statues of naked nymphs and well-endowed males were dotted around in the olive trees and oleanders surrounding the poolside. Marco had brought a large coolbox and produced chilled drinks, glasses, bread, cheese and fruit.

Polly had judged it wise to let Ben play first, before any proper swimming lesson, and he was therefore splashing joyously in the cool green water, wearing a pair of bright blue inflatable armbands and a yellow rubber ring. The three of them were alone. True to his word, Marco had despatched Sophy to his parents' house after breakfast, leaving Angelina the only other person in the farmhouse. The housekeeper, a kind-eyed, warm-hearted woman in her fifties, was already a firm favourite with Ben, since she plied him with sweets whenever Polly's back was turned.

Polly was trying very hard to keep a serene mask, to cover her fury and impotence at being left alone with Marco after what she'd seen last night.

For Ben's sake, she had to keep up an appearance of normality...

'What *what* was like?'

'Being pregnant. Having my baby. Giving birth.' The husky tone of Marco's voice emphasised the intensity of the questions. 'The things I should have known about.'

Polly reached an unsteady hand for her glass of orange juice and took a careful sip.

'If you want to know what childbirth is like, ask Marietta,' she retorted coolly.

'Were you well during your pregnancy?' He appeared to ignore her rebuff, just as he'd ignored her icy attitude all morning.

'Fighting fit. If you really want to know the gory details, I had a normal pregnancy. I took my vitamin pills and folic acid, I went to antenatal classes with Janie for support, I was in labour for twenty-four hours and Ben was delivered by forceps because he got stuck. Luckily he wasn't brain-damaged, as you can see for yourself... Marco, we have to talk...'

'We're talking now. Polly...sweetheart, I can't believe you chose to go through all that alone. If only you'd told me; I'd have been there with you...' There was raw pain in his tense murmur. 'How did you manage afterwards? It must have been hard, on your own...'

She steeled herself not to succumb to the seductive illusion that he cared about her, that he miraculously felt the same consuming love for her that she had always secretly felt for him. If she'd begun to hope, last night had cured her. His emotion was for his son, for the miracle of his coming into the world...and she'd better remember that, or she'd leave herself so vulnerable she'd never be able to cope...

She swallowed, staring at Ben in the pool, thinking about the challenge of those early months of caring for him after he was born, of seeing the other mothers with their enviable, traditional family set-ups, with their loving husbands there to play the part of doting fathers.

Her father had been kind and supportive, and Mary, their housekeeper, had been wonderful, but she'd never be able to blot out the memory of the nights she'd cried into her pillow, yearning to tell Marco, but knowing how it would alienate Sophy and therefore divide the family. She'd spent nearly all of Ben's short life torn apart by her love for Marco and her loyalty to her stepsister—and her fierce determination to compensate for all these shortcomings and do the best she possibly could for Ben...

'I don't mean talk about the past, about pregnancy and childbirth,' she said abruptly. 'I mean about now, about you and me, and Ben...'

'Polly, you excluded me from everything apart from my son's conception. Don't you think I have a retrospective right to know how things were for you?'

'Okay, it was hard, but I was lucky. The moment I saw my baby, I loved him so much there was nothing I wouldn't go through for him. Nothing I wouldn't do to protect him. Do you understand?' She said it through her teeth, in a passionate undertone, in case Ben overheard.

There was silence for a few moments. She turned to look at Marco. He was sipping his iced water slowly, contemplatively. His face was mask-like.

'And you felt you had to protect him from me?'

'I...yes,' she said, drawing a deep, unsteady breath. 'At the time, I thought I had every reason to believe that you'd just be...embarrassed by the situation. I truly believed you were involved with Sophy, and that the responsibility of fathering my child—after such an unplanned, accidental conception—would be the last thing you'd want.

'In...in those circumstances,' she ploughed on, her voice growing more stilted, 'I thought Ben's early formative months would be better spent with just a mother who loved him more than anything in the world rather than in the tense, argumentative situation I imagined would result from telling you about his existence... Oh, Lord, Marco, we've been through all this already...surely you can see why I don't feel I can marry you now?'

'You don't have a choice,' he said, his voice expressionless.

'Yes, I do!' she said in a fierce whisper. Last night's scene on the landing was branded on her brain, making her rigid with pride. 'You can't force me to marry you. You can't use that appalling emotional blackmail on me, either. If you want regular access to Ben, I'm willing to arrange it. But I'm going back to England, and Ben is coming with me. You can visit if you want.'

The look he slowly turned on her made her heart miss a beat.

'Ben stays here. So do you. I've told you, there's no arguing, Polly. We're getting married.' His husky voice was iced with ruthless determination.

'No...'

'I've applied for a court order, stopping you from taking Ben out of Italy.'

'You've *what*...?' Her breath seemed to have entirely left her body.

'I also have your passport, safely stowed away, as extra insurance. And I've spoken to your father, who's overjoyed that we're getting married; it seems the situation has been troubling him for a while. He's suspected for some time who Ben's father is. So you can see there's no point in fighting. You lost your right to independence when you bore my son and hid him from me.'

The calm assertion left her speechless, inwardly churning. He had her *passport*?

'Nothing more you want to talk about?' he prompted, when her silence had lengthened. 'I'll suggest a topic, then, shall I? I'd like to hear about your involvement with Paul.'

She was jolted from her seething reverie. She stared at him blankly. Marco's eyes narrowed on her sudden confusion.

'That's who I assume you were referring to at dinner?' he prompted helpfully. 'When you said that neither of us were free to commit ourselves to marriage.'

'Paul?' she said quickly, thinking rapidly. 'He and I have...have an understanding...'

'Break it off.'

'Your power complex is showing, Marco...' Polly stood up, too tense and drained to continue the fight. Ben was lying on his back, kicking his legs and flailing his arms so much he looked like one of his wind-up bath toys as he made his erratic way from one end of the pool to the other. 'I hope that water isn't as unhygienic as it looks,' she threw back over her shoulder. 'I don't want Ben going down with an ear infection.'

'I had the water replaced two weeks ago. It has an alternative to chlorine in it—safer and less smelly,' Marco said drily.

'Look at me, Mummy! I'm swimming already! Watch me! Watch!'

'You're doing really well, Ben,' she called brightly. 'You'll be managing without the armbands in no time at all...'

'He's a natural.' Marco appeared at her side. He'd stripped down to dark blue swimming shorts. He slid an arm around her shoulders, looking down at her as she stood in her white T-shirt and shorts. 'You must be hot. Why don't you see if that bikini of Marietta's fits you?'

He'd produced one his sister had left hanging on a peg in the summerhouse. It was a very skimpy, exotic, halter-necked creation in white Lycra.

'I'm fine. I'll just watch...'

'As you wish.' Marco went to the side of the pool and strolled to the deep end, poised for a second on the edge, ready to dive. Throat dry, Polly watched him. She'd been in the ultimate intimate situation with him twice, but on neither occasion had she been given the chance to observe, from an interesting distance, the full male glory of his physique; now she couldn't tear her eyes away from him, mesmerised by the matt olive skin, the coarse black hair, the wide shoulders and narrow hips, the long, flat, muscled planes of his body.

He glanced her way just before he dived in, neatly and cleanly, surfacing three-quarters of the way along. She knew he'd seen her staring. She gripped her arms round herself in angry denial.

'Teach me to do that.' Ben was round-eyed with admiration, splashing impatiently. 'Mummy, come in the water as well. Come on, come *on*...!'

'Come on,' Marco echoed with a grin. 'It's relaxing. It'll do you good.'

'Please, Mummy...'

Cursing inwardly, she spun on her heel and marched to the summerhouse. The T-shirt and shorts were swiftly removed and the white bikini fastened in place. She had no mirror to check how it fitted, but, glancing down at herself, she knew that the brief costume revealed far more than she'd ideally choose. The top was slightly padded, pushing her small, high breasts into an unfamiliar sexy cleavage, and the bottoms were cut very high on the leg, making her feel too exposed. At least they weren't thong-style, she reflected, taking a deep breath and emerging from the summerhouse.

Chin high, she walked to the edge of the pool. A low, teasing whistle made her clench her hands at her sides.

'*Bellisima.*' Marco was grinning at her. 'Your mummy is a very beautiful lady, Ben.'

Polly, crimson by now, slid into the water and ducked beneath the silky surface to cool her burning skin. When she came up, scooping handfuls of blonde hair from her eyes, she found herself face to face with Marco. Ben had climbed onto Marco's shoulders and was laughing and flapping his arms like wings, the inflatable bands squeaking madly. Then he grabbed handfuls of Marco's thick black hair, until Marco reached up to lift the small boy into the air, dangling him there while he squealed in delight.

'I'm not going to call you Marco, like Mummy does; I'm going to call you Daddy all the time.' Ben giggled, wriggling like an eel. 'I've wanted a daddy of my own for ages...'

Polly caught her breath. Something deep in her abdomen clenched so hard she felt a pain zigzag right through her body, finishing in a dull ache somewhere near her heart.

She knew what she had to do, and it was in spite of her pride and in spite of her deep distrust of Marco's motives. Ben deserved a chance to grow up in a proper family, with a mother and a father. Seeing father and son together like this, happy and laughing in each other's company, tipped the balance; she loved Ben too much to spoil this for him. And she loved Marco, even though this had to be the most blinkered, inexplicable love that ever existed...

'Louisa said she didn't know why I didn't have a daddy...' Ben was continuing earnestly. 'She said I must have lost him...'

'You've got one now.' Marco grinned up at Ben with such obvious affection that Polly felt her stomach twist with emotion. 'You can tell your friend Louisa that you'd lost him for a while and now you've found him. Okay? *Va bene?*'

'Okay! *Va benny!* Louisa's daddy's funny like you. He says my mummy's beautiful too,' added Ben guilelessly, as Marco lowered him back into the water.

The smile faded from Marco's dark face. He released Ben and watched him dog-paddle proudly away across the pool.

'Louisa's daddy? Is he another reason why you feel you're not free to marry me?' he said under his breath. His eyes were colder suddenly.

She expelled a slow breath.

'Louisa's daddy is married to Louisa's mummy. My dealings with Louisa's daddy are confined to bumping into each other in the village shop,' she informed him, with icy sarcasm. 'But think what you like. I don't care any more...'

'Polly...'

'Actually, Louisa's father reminds me of you,' she added bitingly. 'He couldn't be loyal to one woman to save his life.'

Marco's narrowed stare held a penetrating, interrogative air she was coming to recognise.

'Forgive me if I'm a little confused,' he said slowly, a wry note in his voice. 'Last night I got the feeling you might be more warmly disposed towards me. This morning, so far, you've been treating me like the lowest form of life. What exactly are you basing this latest character assassination on, Polly?'

She blinked at him incredulously. Her heart felt squeezed tightly in her chest. He was dangerously plausible. If she hadn't woken last night and seen what had happened with her own eyes, she'd find it hard not to be taken in.

'You're a brilliant actor, Marco. They say the careers of barrister and actor have a lot in common.' She couldn't keep the shudder of distaste from her voice as she choked back tears. 'Last night you had Sophy in your bedroom. After...oh, God, after telling me you weren't involved with her, leading me to believe that—'

'Polly, wait a minute...' His face had tightened.

'Please...! No more lies! Don't tell me any more lies, Marco. I'm not interested.'

'So what are you saying?' he demanded with soft vehemence. 'That I'm tried and convicted with no defence?'

'I'm saying I really don't *care* what you do.'

'Polly...'

'But I won't fight you any more,' she told him, getting a tight hold on her shattered emotions. 'I will marry you.'

There was a sudden, tense silence. Ben's splashing was the only sound, and that seemed to fade into unreality as they stared at each other.

'You will?' His voice was ominously soft, a dark gleam in his eyes. 'You'll marry me, Polly?'

She stared at him, stunned by the enormity of her decision, but knowing her heart had actually made it, overruling her head, silencing every scrap of common sense she had left...

'For Ben. Yes, I will. You were right. I don't have any choice.' She met his unreadable gaze with furious tears in her eyes.

'Just for Ben...?' Marco's gaze was searching, his eyes suddenly very intense. 'Darling...?'

'Yes. Just for Ben. He needs you; he needs a proper family. I can see now that what I thought was the right thing to do all these years was the wrong thing. I've deprived Ben of his father and I've deprived you of your son, and I have to make up for it...'

And she loved him, a small, betraying voice added inside. She loved him too much to forgo the chance of becoming Mrs Marco Daretta...

'Polly, sweetheart...' The hoarse note in Marco's voice made her heart flip over in her chest, but she held on to her pride. If she gave herself away, if Marco knew how she felt about him, she'd die of humiliation...

'It's right that Ben should know his father. But on one condition...just...just don't come near me when we're alone.'

'Polly, darling...'

She jerked her chin up, her voice shaking. 'I mean it. I'm not sleeping with you again, Marco. Not ever.'

CHAPTER SEVEN

THE marriage of Miss Polly Hamilton to Mr Marco Daretta was, in Polly's opinion, an unnecessarily prolonged and lavish affair.

She stood at the altar in a sleeveless cream shift of bias-cut silk, a circle of cream roses on her upswept hair, reflecting that for someone who was reluctant to get married at all, this was in fact the third ceremony she and Marco had attended. First there'd been the necessary Civil Ceremony in Florence, then a lightning trip to England and a blessing in her local thirteenth-century village church. Now here they were, with great pomp and panache, in a magnificent church in an ancient *piazza* in Florence, exchanging vows with the solemnity of Italian Catholic tradition.

It was her own fault, she knew; she'd refused to get involved in the wedding plans, had left it deliberately to Marco. As a result, Marco and his mother and sisters—the latter at least with uninhibited enthusiasm—had organised this marathon. She suspected it was Marco's way of rubbing her nose in the irony of the situation...

On her left, just behind her, stood her father, tall and distinguished, and, despite this being a Hamilton-Daretta liaison, giving every appearance of approval.

Beside her, Marco was sombre in a black morning suit and cream bow-tie. His best man, Carlo, a quiet black-haired Sicilian cousin, with a brilliantly white smile, stood on Marco's right. Behind them were Janie, Marietta and Angela, Marco's other sister, and her daughter, Rosa, now eight, resplendent in blush-pink silk with pink roses. Ben, proud and frowning in concentration, stood to attention like a small soldier in a replica of his father's outfit.

The pews were nearly full—the groom's side packed with chic, olive-skinned Italians in designer suits and expensive jewellery, the bride's containing far more of her relatives and friends than she'd imagined with such short notice and at such a distance. Their numbers were possibly swelled by Marco's insistence on paying for their airfares and accommodation.

It was cool in the church. Polly was relieved. The heat outside, as they'd walked in procession through the streets in Italian tradition, had been oppressive. Whether through nerves or tension she'd felt nauseous, and her head ached.

She sighed. This was meant to be the happiest day of her life, she thought wistfully. But instead, the very real happiness she was feeling secretly, tightly hidden beneath her surface detachment, was marred by feelings of betrayal and buried anger.

But the happiness was still there; it hovered irrepressibly in the recesses of her mind, ignoring reality, clinging on to a dream of how this momentous day *should* be...

She looked up at Marco as he stood beside her, tall and dark, his strong features expressionless in profile. Her love swelled inside her, clenching her solar plexus, tightening her throat, a bubble of hope which refused to burst. Pride forbade her to show it, but this small core of optimism refused to die... Maybe, if love could overcome all problems, maybe, if Marco loved Ben so much, maybe, if Sophy backed off and gave them space to work things out, then maybe their marriage could turn into the joyful union these vows and ceremonies were all about...

'Are you okay?' Marco's murmur was under his breath.

'Fine. Why wouldn't I be?'

'You look white. Like you're about to pass out.'

'I'm fine.'

'Then at least *try* to resemble a blushing bride,' he whispered bleakly.

She lifted her chin and stared up at the riot of gilded saints and doe-eyed Madonnas lining the wall of the church.

'Sorry. I'll try,' she said in a low, bitter voice. 'I should be feeling grateful, shouldn't I? At least I was spared Sophy as a blushing bridesmaid.'

She sensed rather than saw Marco's thinned mouth and grim gaze.

She was suddenly overcome by claustrophobia. She wanted to turn and run down the aisle, past her family and Marco's, past the wedding guests, out into the *piazza* with its fountain and flowers and views down over the rest of the city. The bitter irony was almost too much. Here was the bride on her wedding day, taking sacred vows before God and the congregation, and all she could do was whisper accusations at her bridegroom.

Tears filled her eyes. She lowered her head, shamed by her own pride and anger. This was for Ben, she told herself silently. For Ben's future, his security, his birthright...

And it was for herself, reminded a small, sharp inner voice. Because she loved Marco...

Later, after what seemed an eternity, they walked from the church into the sun, and Marco's hand closed around hers in a possessive grip that was impossible to break free from.

She looked up at him as the photographer snapped the happy couple on the steps of the church. His eyes looked as black as the shadowed porch behind them. The intensity she saw made her knees go weak.

The bells were clamouring from the tower, startling a flock of white doves into the blue sky overhead.

'You're hurting my hand,' she murmured.

'Sorry.' Marco's smile was bleak as he glanced down at her. He didn't let her go.

The photographer was smiling and shouting something as the guests began to queue up behind them in the church.

'What's he saying?' Polly demanded.

'He wants us to kiss for the camera,' Marco translated wryly. Bending closer, he added, 'We can hardly disappoint him in the circumstances, can we, sweetheart?'

He found her closed mouth and moved his cool lips determinedly over hers, teasing and arousing, until she gasped and he took advantage, kissing her deeply and intimately, capturing her in his arms, the sensuality and hunger so obvious Polly knew it must be there for all to see. She was shaking when he released her. He slid an arm round her shoulders and gave her a smile which made her blink.

'Little hypocrite. You warn me never to touch you again, then you burn in my arms when I kiss you. Look radiant for the photo album, darling,' he advised softly. 'Ben will look at it when he's older, remember?'

She forced herself to smile, shivering with inner rage, but also with a love and a longing that were tearing her apart.

The wedding guests were spilling out around them. They were gradually surrounded by crowds of well-wishers, showered with rice and photographed by dozens of amateur photographers. Polly glanced down at her left hand. The gold band glinted in the sun. Marco's ring. The traditional sign of eternal love between man and woman—or the gold band of ownership Marco insisted on to give his son the security he needed...

Polly wanted it so fervently to be the former that she squeezed her eyes shut for a moment, aiming a silent prayer somewhere into the blue sky above them.

Ironically, when she opened her eyes, Sophy appeared in front of them, in a gold and white Versace suit cut low on the neckline and high on the thigh. Her beautiful face was set in a careful social smile. She was holding Ben by the hand.

'Congratulations,' she said, in a brittle voice. 'I hope you'll both be very happy!'

'Thanks, Sophy.' Marco sounded drily amused.

'Yes. Thank you,' Polly echoed, feeling Marco's hand reach for hers, his fingers tighten once more around it as he held out his other hand to Ben. He bent to lift his son easily with one arm, lodging him on his hip.

'*Ciao.* How's my little man?' Marco grinned.

'Are you my proper daddy now?' Ben demanded, inspecting Marco closely, as if he expected some magical transformation.

'You bet. And now we're going to a party to celebrate.' Marco swept Ben onto his shoulders, and they made their way through the crowds to the waiting Mercedes. Polly smiled up at Ben as she walked beside them. Her heart felt full, nearly bursting with a sad kind of happiness. Whatever she had to endure as Marco's wife, it was worth it to see Ben sparkling with joy like this.

'Be careful with him,' she warned abruptly, as Marco pretended to let him slip and then caught him in mid-air. 'He trusts you totally, for some reason...'

'I'll guard him with my life,' Marco murmured expressionlessly. 'And now you're my wife, I'll do the same for you, *cara mia,*' he added under his breath.

'Sorry?'

'Guard you—' his teeth flashed white as he grinned in the shadows of the car '—with my life.'

'Why does that sound more like a threat than a promise?'

'Paranoia?'

'What's paranoia?' Ben was demanding. 'Mummy, Daddy, what's paranoia...?'

A chauffeur was ushering them into the car, then clicking the door shut on the three of them. They sped through the streets of Florence to the hotel where the reception was to be held. Grateful for Ben's non-stop chatter, intensified after his stint of silence and best behaviour in church, Polly sat very still, stiff and defensive; she wished fiercely that this charade could be over. She just wanted to be alone. She wanted to be back home in Devon, just her and Ben, free from the agony of this situation.

The champagne flowed at the reception, which was held in the courtyard of an old monastery, now turned into a hotel. Round tables beneath huge white Chinese parasols protected the guests from the fierce sun. There were flowers everywhere: on the tables, in stone pots and troughs around the courtyard, and tumbling down the walls—wisterias and honeysuckles.

Polly moved among the chattering crowds in a kind of dream; friends and relatives came to hug and kiss her, exquisite food was circulated on huge silver platters, and through it all Polly smiled and smiled. After a couple of glasses of champagne she almost allowed herself to relax, to believe that she was truly happy, that this marriage to Marco was for real, a lifetime's commitment to love and support one another...

'Satisfied?' Sophy's cool murmur made her jump. Polly was sitting briefly alone at one of the many round tables, and Sophy had slipped into the chair beside her.

Polly turned her head to stare thoughtfully at her stepsister. She didn't have to ask Sophy what she meant; the tone of voice spoke volumes.

'Hardly,' she managed finally. 'Would you be?'

Sophy narrowed her violet eyes. Colour was rising in her cheeks.

'You bet I would! You make me sick, you know that? Since

you've managed the impossible, and got Marco Daretta to the altar, you might at least have the decency to appreciate your luck!' she snapped.

Polly felt the blood drain from her face. She'd been avoiding Sophy as much as possible during the last few weeks. It hadn't been too hard. Since she'd agreed to marry Marco he'd taken himself off to Rome on business, and without Marco around Sophy had found little incentive to visit the farmhouse…

'I'm sorry, Sophy. But Ben's the lucky one,' Polly said woodenly. 'He's got both his parents now…'

'Little miss martyr. You don't fool me, anyway. You've got what you want. You think I don't know you've had a crush on Marco for years?'

Polly's grey-blue eyes were dark with pain as she turned her gaze on her stepsister.

'Sophy, please don't hate me. I didn't plan for this to happen,' she said levelly. 'Why do you think I kept Ben a secret for so long?'

The other girl shrugged stiffly.

'Shame, maybe?' she suggested nastily. 'Maybe you realised poaching your sister's boyfriend by conceiving his love-child wouldn't endear you to the family generally?'

Polly felt herself going hot and cold. She'd known Sophy would feel bitter and angry, but this outburst was far worse than she'd expected. She closed her eyes. When she opened them, she stared past Sophy at the party going on around them.

She could see Ben and Marco in a large group, including several couples in their late twenties or early thirties and a variety of small children, who were milling around and darting between adults' legs and beneath tables.

Her small son, however, was looking very grown-up, proudly holding his father's hand; he had a glass of something which looked like cola in his other hand, his black hair was tousled from much rumpling with his fingers, and he had taken off his jacket and pulled his tie loose.

He was gazing up at Marco, who had done the same thing with his own jacket and tie, and whose black hair wore a remarkably similar appearance to his son's, and was talking and laughing, gesticulating in a very Italian way as he spoke to his friends. It was clear that the subject of his conversation was mainly Ben. Ben's small face was flushed, his dark eyes alight with pleasure and importance at the huge fuss being made over him.

Polly realised that Sophy was following her gaze.

'I can't think why I didn't guess ages ago,' Sophy said lightly, watching the little scenario. 'That he was Marco's, I mean. They're almost identical.'

'I thought you had,' Polly said quietly.

'Well...deep down I half suspected.' Sophy shrugged slightly. She was looking a touch pinker in the face, as if she felt guilty about something.

'There's one thing I just don't understand. In the circumstances, why did you agree to bring him out to Italy?' Polly queried, unable to help herself.

Sophy shot her a veiled glare; she reached inside her soft gold shoulder bag and put a cigarette between her red lips.

'Once Marco asked me, I could hardly refuse.' She paused to flick a slim gold lighter into action, then blew smoke towards Polly. 'Besides, I thought at least being here when the big row was erupting would give me a chance to...to monitor the situation. I hadn't reckoned on Marco's overdeveloped sense of responsibility where children are concerned...'

The bitter cynicism made Polly flinch.

For a second, Marco glanced over and caught her eye; there was a gleam of intimacy, of possessiveness in the look. She could almost see him thinking triumphantly, There's the mother of my son. My wife...

She quenched the foolish lift of her heart. If she just kept her focus on Ben she could make everything else slot into place, she thought determinedly, despite the tangled mess of their relationship.

Already she could see that this was good for Ben; in the space of a few weeks he'd discovered his father, stepped into a new world and acquired a vast quantity of new relatives—including, to Polly's quiet pleasure, a grandmother in the form of her much-loved aunt Ruth.

At another table, she could see her father talking to Ruth and Tino; they were smiling and drinking champagne together. The feud that had poisoned the older generation of the family for so long appeared to be gradually healing. Another good thing...

'Is everything okay?' Marco had come across and had bent down to murmur in her ear. 'I got the impression sisterly love was in short supply over here...'

'We're fine.' Polly smiled up at him brightly, quite unable to stop herself from adding acidly, 'I suppose it must be disconcerting for you to think we might be comparing notes?'

'Notes on what, precisely?' he said quietly. He sat down beside Polly, sliding his arm firmly round her shoulders. His gaze was fixed coldly on Sophy. 'I'm warning you, Sophy; don't interfere in my marriage.'

Polly, even resenting her stepsister's malice as she did, felt a frisson of apprehension down her spine at the steel in Marco's husky voice. Sophy stood up, dragging jerkily on her cigarette. The look she flashed at Polly was venomous.

'Don't worry.' She smiled sweetly, grabbing her bag. 'I only came over to wish Polly luck for the future. I'll leave you two *lovebirds* to enjoy yourselves. Have a wonderful marriage. *Ciao.*'

Polly sat motionless, in the circle of Marco's arm, and watched her sister walk away. Before Sophy disappeared into the crowd, a tall, brown-haired man detached himself from the group Marco had left minutes earlier and intercepted her; he said something, and smiled, showing a flash of white teeth. Sophy stopped in her tracks, replied, and slowly smiled back. They walked together towards a waiter with a tray of champagne, and the man took two glasses off the tray and handed one to Sophy.

'Luciano should keep her out of trouble,' Marco murmured.

Polly looked at him quickly. She felt churned up inside at the unpleasantness of the recent confrontation with Sophy, her feelings a sickening blend of guilt and frustration.

'Who is he?'

'Luciano Lippi. A lawyer. From Pisa. We go climbing together from time to time, sometimes skiing. He's a nice guy. I'll introduce you...'

'Is that how you normally distract your exes when you've no further use for them? Share them around with your friends?'

His gaze was dark, hard to read, as he turned and saw the flash of indignation in her eyes. He was caressing her bare upper arm with his fingers in a way that made her skin break out in goosebumps of awareness. She was mortified to feel her nipples tighten, her breasts sensitise at the same time. Marco's closeness, the clean male scent of his body next to hers, the warm stroking of his fingers on her skin, were combining to undermine her.

'You do my friend an injustice,' he said, with a short laugh. 'Does he look like the kind of man who needs hand-me-downs?'

'No,' she admitted, watching Luciano's attractive profile and attentive manner as he talked to Sophy.

'And besides...Sophy isn't my ex,' Marco went on, his tone a soft drawl.

Polly felt a wave of heat flood her whole body. He didn't have to take such pleasure in reminding her of the sordidness of their situation. The fact that he'd married one sister for access to his son, but intended nothing to change in his relationship with the other... She could hardly believe he could be so cruel. She turned a lidded, simmering gaze on him, blurred through tears of anguish.

'You...*bastard*,' she whispered, her voice catching in her throat.

She stood up and tried to walk away, but he kept hold of her arm. He rose to his feet too, stopping her in her tracks, twisting her back to face him.

'Polly, will you calm down...?' he began. His eyes were black caverns in his taut face.

'Stop it,' she hissed; she was shuddering with suppressed emotion, painfully aware of people all around them, of needing to keep up an appearance of normality, for Ben's sake at least. Marietta and Janie were heading towards them, each carrying a twin, laughing together as they approached. Ben was with them, talking non-stop, asking if he could carry one of the babies...

Polly panicked, blinking away the tears, forcing her face into composure.

'Oh, God, Marco...I can't let Ben see me like this...put your arms round me, pretend you're kissing me or something...'

He held her gaze blankly for a second, then bent closer.

'Whatever you say, sweetheart,' he murmured against her lips, then took her mouth with his and scooped her against him in one sweeping, passionate gesture. To her silent fury he took full advantage of the situation, just as he had outside the church. The kiss was scorching, sexually invasive, his hands roaming down her back and moulding her against his body, branding her his for all to see. She was gasping and breathless when he released her.

'How did I do?' he teased softly. 'Was that convincing enough?'

'Maybe,' she said, her throat dry, 'for people who don't know what's really going on...'

'Count me in their number,' he murmured drily.

She stared up at him, drowning in the dark well of his eyes, and in spite of everything she was glad of the circle of his arm to support her as Ben bounced up and Marietta and Janie reached them.

'Can't you wait until your honeymoon?' Marietta teased.

Marco grinned, slanting a look at Polly which made her colour rise. He released her slowly and bent down to lift Ben up, greeting his son with such an air of worshipful pride Polly found herself smiling shakily.

'Ciao, mio figlio,' he said, laughing at Ben's serious little face on a level with his, and tweaking his nose.

'Ciao, Papà.' Ben copied the nose tweak on Marco, making everyone laugh.

'Are you going to be well behaved for your grandma and Aunt Marietta while I take your *mamma* on honeymoon?'

'Of course he is,' Marietta said, ruffling Ben's hair. 'He's going to help me look after the twins.' Ruth had offered to look after Ben, and Marietta was moving up to Ruth and Tino's farmhouse for the week because her husband was going to be away on business.

'I'm going to help to bath them,' Ben added, nodding vigorously. 'Mummy, what's a honeymoon?'

'Well...' Polly floundered.

'It's a holiday people have when they've just got married, because usually they're very tired afterwards,' Janie supplied, eyeing Polly's air of fevered tension with a hint of concern. 'And looking at you, Poll, a holiday is long overdue...'

'Don't worry,' Marco told Janie with a faint grin, 'I'll make sure she relaxes.'

'You have to stay in bed all the time,' Ben announced, his eyes wide with innocence. 'My friend Louisa said her big sister stayed in bed all day for two weeks on her honeymoon...'

In the short silence that followed one of the babies gurgled, and waved her arms around windmill fashion; her twin sister copied, and everyone laughed again.

'Ben's friend Louisa is a fount of information,' Marco murmured to Polly, his grin lopsided. 'Who the hell is she?'

'A little girl at playgroup. She's four.'

'Four going on fourteen.' Janie laughed.

'I think it's time we left,' Marco suggested, hugging Ben. 'Our flight leaves in an hour. Okay, little one? Can you spare me your mummy for a week?'

'Grandad Tino said I can have chocolate ice cream milkshake every morning for breakfast.' Ben shrugged with a reassuring air of security. 'I'll be okay.'

Polly gazed at her son, her heart contracting even while she smiled brightly. Over the past few weeks Ben had allowed himself to be absorbed into the Daretta family like a willing drop of water on a sponge. It was a case of mutual adoration between Ben and his new grandparents. After more than three years of being the most important adult in his life, she could see that this was healthy. It was just hard to accept...

'Va bene?' Marco confirmed softly.

'Si, va bene, Papà,' Ben agreed, proudly displaying his newly acquired scrap of Italian.

The identical eyes met in silent union. Polly knew it was ridiculous to feel excluded, but she did.

The flight to Trapani, in Sicily, was quite short. Polly sat in a window seat of the small twelve-seater plane, her face carefully averted from her new husband, and watched Italy skimming along far below them.

Marco had insisted they take a traditional honeymoon. No amount of resistance would deter him. In his words, it would cement their marriage in the eyes of their family and friends, and it would kill gossip about the nature of their relationship.

'I'm taking you to Sicily,' he'd stated flatly. 'I have some friends who own a villa on Favignana.'

'Favignana?' She'd stared at him, half-curious, half-resentful.

'It's a little island off the west coast. It's quiet and we can have some privacy there.'

'Who wants privacy?' she'd dismissed coldly. 'If we have to go anywhere on honeymoon I'd prefer somewhere noisy.'

Somewhere with crowds of people, where they could avoid intimate conversations, where they could be distracted and entertained without spending any time together, she'd thought, seeing the flash of grim amusement in Marco's eyes and setting her teeth. It seemed to be a one-sided fight so far: Marco behaving with perfect courtesy, being mature and infuriatingly considerate, and her feeling goaded into childish retaliation to hide how much she was hurting inside.

They'd been shopping in Florence; he'd been determined for her to acquire the kind of wardrobe suited to his wife-to-be. She'd gone along with this spending spree just as she'd gone along with the rest of the wedding preparations, outwardly detached, but inwardly either screaming with indignation, or, every now and then, glowing secretly with excitement and—most shameful of all—a confused kind of pleasure. However hurt or angry or emotionally confused she was feeling, to be marrying Marco, whatever the circumstances, had been her dream for so long...

She'd chosen the wedding dress with Ruth, Janie—who'd flown out as soon as she'd heard—and Marietta. But with Marco she'd resignedly succumbed to pressure and bought dresses and suits, long and short skirts, shirts and figure-hugging tops, silk and satin lingerie in delectable shades of gold and ivory and smoke-blue, shoes, bags and jewellery.

She glanced down now at the tight little skirt she was wearing, cut with wonderful designer simplicity in a stretchy white and deceptively expensive material which lovingly hugged the shape of her slender hips and thighs, and at the figure-moulding black top, cap-sleeved and low-necked, with a deeply scooped back. With low black thong-sandals, and one of the simple gold pendants Marco had advised her to choose, the outfit set off her golden tan and sun-bleached hair—both of which she'd acquired in the past few weeks, swimming daily with Ben in Marco's pool.

She felt quite different; very European, very...Italian. Devon, her old life there, her business, which Janie had offered to temporarily take over for her, all seemed centuries away.

She smoothed her skirt with her hands. The gold rings on her third finger glittered at her. The engagement ring Marco had chosen was simple, but shockingly expensive: a conventional diamond, large and round and many-faceted to reflect the light. The wedding band was smooth and rounded, very traditional. Marco's was a wider, heavier version of the same. It gleamed on his left hand as she glanced involuntarily across.

'Are you going to share your thoughts with me?' Marco enquired, a note of wry challenge in his voice. He'd attempted to make conversation when they first got on the plane, but she'd answered in monosyllables and he'd given up, and immersed himself in reading some legal documents out of a small attaché case.

'You really wouldn't want to know,' she said coolly.

'We've sat in total silence for thirty minutes.' he pointed out, his mouth twisting. 'Try me.'

'I was just willing the next seven days to pass as quickly as possible.'

'Not a romantic attitude to your honeymoon, *Signora* Daretta.'

'It was your idea. We could quite easily have done without this charade...'

'We agreed that for Ben's sake this marriage is going to look genuine,' said Marco expressionlessly, lifting a hand to attract the air hostess who was serving drinks. 'Newly-wed couples have honeymoons.'

'We could have found an excuse...'

'Ben is going to have a whale of a time being spoiled rotten by my parents. We're going to have a week's holiday.' He spelled out the words deliberately slowly, his voice harder. 'Which will give us both some breathing space, during which we can agree some kind of peace treaty.'

'Yes. Quite. As long as I keep reminding myself that this is for Ben's sake, I can keep down the waves of nausea,' she said in a low, unsteady voice.

Marco dropped his cool air of control for a second and shot her a look of dark, unguarded pain.

'You really know how to maximise an insult,' he said huskily. 'Just what the hell did Sophy say to you at the reception?'

'Why?' She was making fists of her hands in her lap, she saw, looking down at the white of her knuckles. The look in Marco's eyes was making her stomach hollow and her heart pound.

'Because you've been behaving like this ever since I interrupted your cosy conversation.'

The hostess, a beautiful olive-skinned Italian girl, was hovering at Marco's side. Her dark eyes were bright with feminine interest as she studied his lean good looks, watched the way he impatiently raked back his thick black hair. He raised an eyebrow at Polly. 'What do you want to drink?'

'Nothing, thank you.'

'My wife will have a dry white wine. I'll have a whisky. Ice no water,' he ordered in Italian. 'Thanks.'

He took a hefty swig of his drink before he looked back at Polly. She was ignoring the glass of white wine in front of her and feeling rather childish again in doing so.

'Well?' he prompted, harshly. 'Am I right? Was Sophy stirring up trouble again?'

'If your guilty conscience is troubling you, you can hardly blame me,' she said jerkily. 'Sophy merely pointed out the truth.'

'And what's that?' His dark eyes held a grim glitter.

'That poaching her boyfriend by conceiving his love-child was hardly designed to improve family relations.'

Marco said something that sounded very rude in Italian, under his breath. He took another drink and closed his eyes briefly. When he opened them, he fixed Polly with an intent, lidded stare.

'I said I would not keep on defending myself against false accusations,' he said at last. 'There doesn't seem much point, since you've made it clear you don't trust me. But just one more time, Polly. Sophy is not my girlfriend. Whatever she has told you over the years, she has never been my girlfriend...'

'But I saw you together, that Easter in Prizzi. I saw you kissing that last night. And ever since Sophy's made no secret about your love affair—how you ring her and stay with her and buy her presents and invite her to Italy....'

'Listen to me...' He drank some more whisky, his mouth set in a grim line. 'This is not easy to say; it sounds crude, and disloyal to your stepsister. Sophy has always made it clear that she would like us to be lovers. That Easter in Prizzi, yes, she was flirting with me...'

'You flirted right back.' Polly was going hot and cold, distraught at the pain of talking about it. 'The two of you went out together for meals all the time...'

'Only because you declined to join us.' Marco gave her a half-smile, inspecting her hot cheeks with a considering glint in his eyes. 'You were the visiting English cousins; my parents were overjoyed at the contact with the Hamilton side of the family. What was I supposed to do? Tell Sophy she wasn't my type and send her to her room to read a magazine for the duration of your visit?'

'Sophy talked of no one else all the way back to England,' Polly said in a low voice. 'She told me how you'd slept together that night before she left, and how you were going to stay in touch...'

'It's not true, Polly. I didn't sleep with her. I wanted us to be friends, not enemies.' Marco sounded weary suddenly. 'Can't you understand that? Faced with the first olive branch in a long-running family feud, knowing how much reconciliation meant to my mother, do you think I wanted to wreck everything by telling Sophy to get lost? She made it clear enough she wanted a sexual relationship when she turned a friendly kiss on the cheek into that kiss you saw. I tried to let her down gently, but then I encouraged the friendship, to cause the least damage to family relations...'

'It all sounds so plausible,' Polly heard herself saying, in a tight, controlled voice. 'But don't forget I've seen the two of you together quite recently, Marco. I saw the way you hung around together in the gardens the night Ben arrived. I saw how Sophy clung to you when you appeared at the garden door. And I saw you...' she swallowed on a sudden, bitter lump in her throat '...I saw you inviting her into your bedroom that night, when presumably you were confident I was fast asleep.'

Marco gazed at her for a long moment, his eyes bleak.

'If I told you she came to my room and demanded to know the whole story about you and me and Ben, looking as if she was about to have hysterics if I didn't let her in, I suppose you wouldn't believe that, either?'

Polly bit her lip. She was trembling. She longed to believe him, but the void of suspicion and pride inside felt like a physical pain.

'I don't know,' she whispered miserably. 'I don't know what to think, what to believe.' She didn't know what she *dared* to believe. If she started trusting him, he could destroy her...

'*Cara...*' He reached to take her hand, imprisoning her fingers in his.

'Don't! Don't call me that...' She turned tear-blurred eyes on him, wishing she were anywhere but on a public plane in full view of several interested passengers. 'So what...what did you mean, when you said at the reception that Sophy wasn't your ex? Was that a slip of the tongue, then?'

'Polly...' Marco's voice had deepened to hoarse incredulity. 'To qualify as my ex she would have had to be my girlfriend at one time...' He turned a narrowed gaze on her and she almost flinched at the glitter of icy disbelief she saw there. 'That's what I meant. What did you think? You thought I was planning to continue an affair with her? You thought I'd say that to you, plan such a thing, on our wedding day?'

She swallowed convulsively.

'Yes.'

There was a resounding silence.

'You really do despise me, don't you?' he said at last, very quietly.

She couldn't think what to say. Abruptly, the conversation seemed to have taken a nightmare turn. 'It's hard to believe the kind of man you think I am,' he went on. 'Are you so suspicious, so untrusting with every man you meet? Or is this because of who I am?'

She blinked at him, not understanding at first.

'Because of who you are?'

'I'm a Daretta, remember?' he taunted bitterly. 'Capable of anything. Even, as your grandmother used to think, of criminality.'

'Don't bring that stupid family feud into this again,' she shot back. 'You saw your parents and my father at our wedding reception, talking together, being friendly. Everyone wants to forget about it except you! And if I misunderstood what you said, then...then, I'm sorry...'

He turned away, picking up his whisky glass and downing the rest of its contents.

'So am I,' he said flatly.

She watched his set, remote profile as he picked up the sheaf of documents and began to read. Lost in misery, she realised that in a few deft seconds he'd twisted their argument and put her totally in the wrong.

She was so confused; she didn't even know how she felt any more.

Staring out of the small window of the aircraft, she choked back angry, frustrated tears. The coming week seemed an endless ordeal.

CHAPTER EIGHT

THE villa on Favignana was a small, whitewashed building, rustic and simple, perched on its own above a sandy beach. An outside stone staircase was the only access to the upper level. Here, sun-loungers, white-slatted chairs and a white-painted table were scattered around a large terrace bounded by low white walls, offset by massive stone urns of scarlet geraniums. Beneath an overhanging porch a long pine sofa, upholstered in sea-green and white flowered cotton, occupied a place against the outside wall.

One big flagstoned room, visible to Polly as she peered inside via an open shutter, seemed to provide kitchen, dining and sitting areas all in one. She could see a pine table and chairs, two arm-chairs, white candles in wrought-iron wall-sconces, and a white-washed fireplace full of pine cones and shells.

The lower level was where the bedrooms were. She hadn't seen those yet. Marco had taken their cases in while she'd climbed up here, curious to see the view from the highest point, and, if she was honest, anxious to delay the awkward intimacy of seeing their sleeping quarters and any potential battle of wills over separate bedrooms...

Slightly out of breath, she found herself gazing down at a wide expanse of turquoise and navy blue sea, cliffs dotted with low-growing green shrubs and a pale half-moon of sand. She breathed in deeply, trying to relax. The air was warm and heavy, the sun was blazing on her face, and the singing of the cicadas was deafening.

'Do you like it?' Marco had silently come to stand behind her. She tensed at his nearness.

'It's not what I expected.'

'Why?'

She shrugged. 'I was imagining...something grander.'

'I thought you enjoyed the simple life. Cliff-walks, collecting

132

shells, that kind of thing? Would you have preferred a plush hotel?'

'No!' She swung round, frowning, 'I didn't mean that at all. I love it...' She stopped.

She'd been thinking that it didn't seem like Marco's style. But what did she really know about his taste in getting away from it all? Just because he spent a lot of his time being a high-powered barrister in London and Rome, it didn't necessarily follow that he craved luxury in his leisure time. But she couldn't imagine Sophy here, she reflected involuntarily. Sophy's taste ran to marble foyers, international cuisine, satellite TV in every bedroom...

She was holding her breath, wishing she hadn't blurted out her feelings and wishing he wasn't standing quite so close. She found herself within a few inches of his body.

'You love it?' he questioned quietly. 'Do you think you could ever learn to love me, Polly?'

Her heart seemed to stop.

She couldn't speak. She just stared up at him mutely while her heart began thudding deafeningly.

'What kind of question is that?' she managed finally, her throat constricted. She was floundering now, totally taken aback by the directness, the openness of this question. 'How can you *learn* to love someone?'

'Arranged marriages still happen in many countries. If two strangers can learn to love each other, there's hope for us. We're far from strangers, Polly. And we've got the strongest incentive in the world.'

'Ben.'

He nodded slowly, his expression deadpan.

Heat crept up her body.

'Emotional blackmail? If I care about Ben, I must learn to love his father? It might be better if we were strangers, Marco,' she managed huskily, her eyes very bright with anger. 'Then I'd have no special reason to distrust you.'

'I could try teaching you to trust me.'

With a sharpness in her voice, she said quickly, 'You're a very busy man. I'm sure you've better things to do than waste your valuable time, Marco.'

'Not at all. For the next seven days I can waste as much time as I like.' He slowly took hold of one of her hands. He linked their fingers, then lifted her hand to inspect her small fingers entwined with his. She swallowed in silent turmoil.

'On the plane, I thought you weren't speaking to me,' she said, her voice trembling.

'Brooding on insults is no way to start a honeymoon.'

'This isn't a conventional honeymoon.'

He raised his eyebrows, his eyes bleakly amused. 'What's a conventional honeymoon?'

He was drawing her towards the steps, his grip on her hand unrelenting as he led the way down to the lower level of the villa, guided her round the door. Propelled inside, she blinked in the dimness of the shuttered room. Extracting her hand from Marco's, she walked in and inspected her surroundings in growing bewilderment.

It took her a few moments of investigation to assimilate that the lower level of the villa appeared to comprise only one large bedroom, with an adjoining white-tiled bathroom.

In the muted, filtered light, she saw that the bedroom was square, a high-ceilinged, white-walled room, with an enormous pine-framed bed. The bed was made up with crisp white sheets, tucked in tightly with military precision and folded back and smoothed to creaseless perfection, and a sea-green bedspread in some rough, woven cotton material. On both sides of the bed cream fur rugs lay on the floor, and cream-shaded reading lamps stood on small pine lockers. A huge fan whirred hypnotically on the pine-planked ceiling. Her suitcase stood, as if making some kind of audible statement, alongside Marco's, by the long pine chest of drawers under the window.

Polly stood rooted to the stone-flagged floor. Marco had gone to open the windows, then to push back the slatted wooden shutters. Sunlight streamed in, dazzling her. The big windows looked out over the sea and French doors opened onto another terrace, with more geraniums in urns. In a homely touch, a white plastic washing-line had been strung between two pine trees, with a few red and yellow pegs swaying in the slight breeze.

'I don't know about you, but I'm thirsty,' Marco said calmly, opening what looked like a cupboard door and revealing a small fridge stocked with bottles of mineral water, white wine, bottled beer, fruit juice and half an enormous pink watermelon, wrapped in cling film. Something looking suspiciously like a bottle of champagne stood in the door compartment.

'What would you like?' Another cupboard door hid a row of glasses, dishes, some cutlery.

'Just...water, please.' Polly cleared her throat and sat down abruptly on the bed. 'Marco, is this the only bedroom?'

'Yes. Do you want to take a shower or something before we unpack?' Marco handed her a glass of iced water.

She drank some, her hand trembling as she held the glass.

'You're expecting us to sleep in the same bed? All week?'

He drained a glass of water in one thirsty gulp, then strolled to the other side of the bed and lay down experimentally. He gave a small bounce on the mattress.

'It's king-size, and it's quite comfortable,' he pronounced expressionlessly. 'Expensive—pocket-sprung, I'd say. You won't bounce up and down when I turn over. Maybe not designed to international orthopaedic standards, but—'

'I don't care if it's king-size, dwarf-size, pocket-sprung or *whatever*,' snapped Polly, driven beyond cool control. 'I am not sleeping in the same damn bed with you all damn week! Got it?'

He got up, stretched slightly, and headed for the bathroom.

'If you're in no hurry,' he said casually, 'do you mind if I go first?'

She closed her eyes and drank her water, counting in her head.

When she opened her eyes, Marco had disappeared. The hiss of the shower was faintly audible through the closed door of the bathroom.

Polly stood up and paced around the bedroom, mentally examining her options. She went out onto the terrace and gazed frustratedly at the glimpse of cobalt-blue sea, glinting in the afternoon sun, trying to suppress a hint of hysteria. She was going hot and cold at the thought of sleeping in that big bed with Marco every night for the next week. The effort of hiding her feelings in such forced intimacy would leave her horribly vulnerable...

She shivered. Marco had no right to put her in this impossible, embarrassing situation. She'd made her provisos, hadn't she? She'd spelled out her terms when she'd agreed to marry him. She would just have to insist that one of them slept elsewhere...

'Sorry to be so long.' Marco interrupted her fierce reverie, stroking light, possessive hands down her arms as he appeared beside her. 'Your turn, sweetheart. A shower will revive you.'

She blinked at the sight of him, an unsettling vision of lean, male virility in a brief, hip-hugging white towel; snatching up her toiletries case from the bedroom, she bolted for the bathroom, shutting the door thankfully as she attained the safe haven. Her relief was short-lived. There wasn't even a lock on the door, she registered, appalled. She burst out again, protesting, only to find Marco stark naked, towelling his hair. He paused, smiling in slow amusement at her hot, flustered face.

'Problem?'

'The door doesn't lock. For heaven's sake, put some clothes on...'

He didn't move, lifting an eyebrow in an infuriating way.

'Why? It's not cold. And we are a married couple now. Married couples are allowed to walk around their bedrooms with no clothes on, remember?'

Holding her breath to control her temper, she turned and marched back into the bathroom, and slammed the door furiously.

'Just don't you dare come in here,' she shouted, peeling off the black top and white skirt, stepping out of her brief thong panties. She switched on the shower and plunged beneath the spray to cool her burning skin.

'Relax,' Marco called back. 'My mother taught me it's rude to burst in when a lady is in the bathroom.'

Thank God for Aunt Ruth, Polly told herself, beginning to see the funny side of her overreaction. She deliberately took her time. She shampooed her hair twice, conditioned it, used scented shower gel, shaved her legs, and was just contemplating a herbal face-mask when there was a light tap on the door.

'You can't stay in there all week, Polly.'

'I wasn't planning to...' she retorted stiffly. Wrapping herself in a vast white towel, she cautiously opened the door. Marco stood there, a dark gleam in his eyes. He still wore only the small white towel round his hips. As she tried to slip past him he caught her in his arms and cradled her there, her body held against him with a force like gentle steel.

'You smell delicious,' he breathed against her neck, letting his tongue slide sensuously against her throat.

'Marco, stop it...' She shivered violently.

'Your skin's like warm silk...'

'This is not fair,' she hissed, her voice breaking as he stepped backwards, steering her towards the bed. 'Marco, let go of me. You promised...'

'I didn't promise anything,' he murmured grimly, succeeding neatly in collapsing them both onto the bed and moving rapidly to pin her there as she began to thresh her arms and legs and roll away from him. 'Apart from my promises in church today...'

'We both know they meant nothing...' She felt her throat choking with unshed tears as he unwound the towel from her breasts and stroked his fingers gently over her tightening nipples.

'Don't speak as if you know my mind,' he warned softly, pushing the towel off her completely and kneeling up to survey his catch. 'I wouldn't presume to read yours...'

'I said I'd marry you but not sleep with you,' she said, trembling with the urgency of her pride. 'You knew those were my... You knew that, Marco. I thought you...I thought you would respect my feelings...'

'I can't,' he breathed hoarsely, a shudder going through his body; he was smoothing his hands down the length of her, his eyes following his hands. 'I can't be with you and not want to make love to you...'

'Oh, Marco...oh, dear God...' She kept her eyes wide open, tried to use her pent-up anger to control the wave of passion and desire he was creating. It didn't seem to have any effect; her body was starting to betray her, just the way it always did when Marco touched her and held her. Her response to him felt like a dark pit of longing opening up inside her, clamouring to be filled, deaf and blind to intellectual reason.

'Admit that you feel the same...'

'No...'

He deliberately raked his fingers down her stomach and slid two knowing fingers between the silky curls at the apex of her thighs, his eyes dark slits on her face as he met the satiny warmth of her arousal.

'No?' His voice was hoarse with desire, the intensity of his passion setting her on fire. 'You say you don't want me, but you respond like this when I touch you...?'

'It's just a physical thing...' she managed, on a suppressed groan of hunger and shame. 'Oh...oh...please...Marco...'

'Do you have this "physical thing" with men in general?' His mouth was moving hungrily now on her breasts, trailing kisses over her stomach, his fingers and hands caressing with intoxicating strokes, exploring deeper, with growing intimacy. 'Or just with me, my darling?'

'Just...oh, please...just with you...'

'Polly...sweetheart...' The catch of masculine emotion in his deep voice made every tiny nerve-ending come alive; she was utterly seduced. She looked up at him, focusing intently on his dark face, shaking uncontrollably with passionate hunger.

'Oh, God, Marco...' she whispered helplessly, touching his face with shaky fingers, slowly and possessively tracing the hard line of cheekbone and jaw, feeling the tension and heat in his body. 'I don't know how to resist you...'

'Then don't, my darling...' He breathed the words on a hoarse, choked outbreath; she found her eyes locked with his, and a communication never achieved in words seemed to take place in that shared gaze, lidded ink-black with wide grey-blue, an emotional communion triggering the wildest, deepest desire inside her, stark and hungry, like sweet savagery...

With a small convulsion of her body, she reached to pull him to her, opening herself in mindless need, feeling his body jerk and violently shudder in response and thrust to fill her with abrupt, tight possession. She heard his hoarse groan of victory, heard herself gasp and cry out with uninhibited pleasure and surrender, as the pace and intensity quickened and spiralled and sexual desire took over completely.

'This you have to taste to believe.' Marco put the dish of spaghetti Bolognese down on the table between them with a theatrical flourish.

'Does that mean it's good or bad?' She sniffed delicately at the enticing aroma, smiling slightly in the candlelight. It smelled wonderful.

Marco, looking relaxed and in control, in jeans and loose white T-shirt, had insisted on playing chef tonight. She'd been relegated to table-laying.

He raised an eyebrow but otherwise ignored her teasing. Instead he slung the teatowel over his shoulder and twisted the corkscrew into the cork of a bottle of wine, extracting it with a professional 'plop'.

'If the *Signora* would care to taste the wine?'

'If *il patrone* recommends it, that's fine by me.'

They were eating at the white-slatted table on the terrace, by the light of a large anti-mosquito candle. The night air felt very warm, even in the thigh-short, clingy eau-de-nil dress she wore, low-backed and strappy. All around them, the darkness and the silence were unbroken.

'We could be alone in the world here,' she murmured, watching the aromatic steam rising from the spaghetti as Marco dished a portion onto her plate.

'Apart from half a dozen owls and about twenty million cicadas and crickets. Not to mention the mosquitos.'

'I wasn't counting animal and insect life.'

'You should. All God's little creatures.' He reached across suddenly and slapped her quite hard on the arm.

'Ouch! Why...? Oh, yuck...!' A squashed mosquito was unceremoniously flicked to the terrace. Marco laughed.

'Sorry. I think I caught him before he bit. I told you to spray yourself,' he reminded her calmly. 'A Sicilian mosquito never misses his chance.'

'Sounds rather like a certain Sicilian man I know... Anyway, I did put some of that repellent on...'

'It just shows how irresistible you are. It must have been a male...'

Catching the glint in his eyes, she lowered her eyes to her plate and took a mouthful of spaghetti.

Their ungovernable passion earlier had knocked her out completely for a couple of hours; when she'd finally woken, Marco had brought her chilled champagne and fed her tiny slivers of watermelon. She adored fruit, and especially watermelon. She couldn't remember anything more sensual and tender and utterly overwhelming than his apparent total concentration on her physical well-being; they'd ended up making love again, long and slow and agonisingly pleasurable, tasting of champagne and watermelon...

'We need to talk,' he said, when they'd both nearly finished their spaghetti and polished off the bottle of red wine.

'Life would be much simpler if we didn't,' Polly said slowly.

'If we just communicated by physical union?' Marco leaned back in his chair and shot her a wolfish grin. 'Like animals? You may have something there...'

'Whenever we talk...seriously talk, I mean...there are too many obstacles.'

'I agree, it's risky. That doesn't mean the solution is to ignore them.'

'We finish up saying horrible things and falling out,' she pointed out, pushing her spoon and fork together and draining her wineglass. 'That was really excellent, Marco. Spaghetti Bolognese is one of my favourite meals. Next time I'll cook for you—some of that English home cooking you said you love. How about roast pork with all the trimmings? Stuffing, apple sauce, buttered cabbage, carrots, runner beans, gravy...'

'I'll hold you to that. So, we should pretend all is well and no obstacles exist?' He ignored her determined effort to switch subjects. 'One of the reasons I insisted on this week away together was so we could talk about our future. There are things we should discuss,' he persisted, standing up and carrying their plates inside. 'Fresh peaches, ice cream, or tiramisu?' he called back, examining the contents of the pre-stocked fridge and freezer.

'Peaches, please...'

He reappeared with a bowl of peaches, two plates and a sharp knife, and set about peeling the fruit.

'So you want to talk about...us?' she reminded him warily.

'Us. Ben. What we want for him. Our...commitment to each other....'

He handed her a slice of peach and she put it in her mouth. It was cool and juicy, but her enjoyment was hindered by a mounting wave of panic as she tried to interpret his words and the meaning behind them.

'I want Ben to grow up happy and healthy...' she began cautiously.

Marco bit into his own slice of peach and sat back in his chair, his eyes darkening. 'I want that too. That's why I'm working so hard at making sure Ben has both his parents around.'

She sucked in her breath.

'Is it such hard work?' she heard herself asking.

A glimmer of a smile touched his mouth. 'I think you know the answer to that.'

She wriggled uncomfortably in her chair. Somehow these conversations with Marco always made her feel guilty, or, even worse, petty and selfish, and that made her angry. It was as if he was the one who felt he had to forgive her, not the other way around.

'It's hardly proved easy so far, has it?' he added, gently ironic.

That depended on what he was talking about, she thought wryly; getting her into bed had proved humiliatingly easy.

'Hardly surprising, in the circumstances.' Her tone sounded shorter than she'd intended. 'I know this is...this is all for Ben's sake,' she amended more quietly. 'It's just that...whenever we talk like this, I feel like you're judging me for what happened in the past, and...and I don't feel you have the right to do that.'

Marco studied the peach stones on the plate. After a pause, he said slowly, 'What were you going to tell Ben? He'd already begun asking questions, hadn't he?'

She nodded stiffly.

'I told him his...his father lived in a foreign country...'

'Only partially true.'

'And that he...' she swallowed on a sudden lump of emotion '...he loved him very much, but he was a very busy man...'

The bleakness had flared to banked-down anger.

'Great. So Ben was going to grow up thinking his father was

far too busy to ever come to see him? For the love of God, Polly…did you never stop to think that babies of three grow up into enquiring adults?'

'Don't patronise me.'

'Okay, so you did think about that. So you know that when you're an adult knowing where you come from, who your mother and father are, the circumstances of your conception—all the things that at the time maybe don't seem so important to a baby—they are what you build your whole life on. Knowing whether or not your parents love you is the most important thing in the world, Polly.'

'I know that!' She felt very near to tears. 'There's no need to…to lecture me on the responsibilities of parenthood, Marco!'

'I'm sorry…I wasn't meaning to sound like I was lecturing. I was trying to make you understand how I feel,' he said on a long outbreath, as if he'd got his anger back under control. 'I want to tell you something that happened to a friend of mine, Luis, a guy I met at university. He was twenty-two before he found out about his real father. He'd often wondered why the man he thought of as his father appeared to dislike him intensely but got on well with his other two sons. He heard the truth from his mother, just before she died prematurely. His father was a Spanish fisherman she'd had a brief affair with while she was married; the husband found out, said he'd bring up the boy as his own, but had never managed to overcome his anger enough to love him…'

'Marco, that's so sad…' Polly was clenching her hands, her heart shrinking at the bleakness of the story.

'Luis's real father knew about him, but he had no money—nothing to offer a child except a father's unconditional love. Just before she died, Luis's mother finally gave him a pile of letters she'd received over the years and hidden from her husband, and an address and a telephone number in Spain. He rang the number and the man confirmed that he had a son in England. He then broke down in tears and said he'd been waiting all his life for that telephone call. Luis went to visit him, and he told me afterwards that for the first time in his life he felt he belonged somewhere. He felt ''connected''. His father took him in his arms and hugged him, and that was the first time he'd ever known a father's hug. He had his father's eyes, build, hands; he said they sat and cried like babies for the first half an hour.'

'Thank God they met.' Polly gave a short laugh to hide her emotional turmoil. 'I thought you were leading up to some dreadful tragic ending—his father dying before he could meet him or something...'

'Luis's tragedy was that he grew to adulthood without his father's love and support.' Marco shrugged. 'His father wasn't well when they met. He died six months later. Luis could only reflect on twenty-two wasted years. He had a mini-nervous breakdown, flunked his finals, and spent the next few years seeing a counsellor. Maybe it depends on how you look at things, Polly...'

'Yes. Yes, I do see...' She let out a shaky breath, and rubbed her hands over her face again.

'What happened to Luis could easily have happened to me. My mother was under huge family pressure to cut ties with my father, marry a well-connected Englishman.'

She met Marco's eyes and their gazes held with painful knowledge and understanding, as years of family feuding and resentment swirled behind the impact of the words.

'So you see,' he said quietly, 'I have a lot of incentive to fight for my son.'

With what Polly later reflected as diabolical timing, a mobile phone shrilled through the pause, shattering the silence that had abruptly descended.

Marco pulled a wry face, and went to retrieve it from the kitchen.

'I meant to turn this thing off,' he murmured, flipping open the mouthpiece and abruptly stating his name.

'Soph...' He dropped his voice, turned away from Polly, and walked back into the villa. The one-sided conversation sounded cool, quite terse and uncompromising, but she knew, she just knew it was Sophy. Sophy had his mobile phone number. Sophy—beautiful, angry, vindictive Sophy—who felt able to ring him on his honeymoon...

Polly felt the familiar sick feeling in the pit of her stomach.

The pain of rejection and humiliation lay just around the next corner; she sensed it with a drying throat and an ache in her heart. For all Marco's high-minded talk of fatherhood and commitment, he was prepared to run the risk of carrying on his affair with Sophy...

Marco came back to join her a few moments later. There was a loaded pause as he met her eyes.

'That, I gather, was Sophy?' Polly queried expressionlessly.

'Yes...' Marco expelled a long breath and sat down heavily.

'Is everything all right in Tuscany?' she went on quickly. 'Ben's all right?'

'Yes, yes, Ben's fine, Polly...'

'And your mother is fine? Your father? Your sisters? There are no crises in Daretta family life back in Tuscany?'

His face had darkened, a glitter of hard awareness in his eyes as he watched her white-faced anger across the table.

'Polly...'

'So how come Sophy has your mobile phone number?' she pressed on, the words forming themselves with cool precision. 'How come she feels able to ring you during your honeymoon, Marco?'

'The answer to that is I'm not sure how Sophy got my mobile number; she must have rung my office and got it from my assistant,' Marco said quietly. 'Polly, don't look like that—knowing Sophy, she was probably enjoying the knowledge that she'd be causing trouble by ringing me tonight. But she was actually ringing about a legal problem—she reneged on a modelling contract to help me, by bringing Ben to Italy...'

Polly stared at him, seeing but not seeing the hard, attractive features, the steady dark blue gaze. She felt as if a red mist had risen in front of her eyes and had simultaneously clouded her ability to hear. She couldn't fight the pain of suspicion and jealousy; it tore like a knife-wound inside. Marco's words, his explanations all sounded plausible. But with every new instance of Sophy's involvement in his life her will to trust him faltered. The worm of doubt slithered again into her mind, poisoning her brief illusion of happiness, her vision of how their relationship could be...

'You were saying, earlier, that we needed to talk about our commitment to each other. I understand you perfectly now. You mean you want to discuss how, even now we're married, and regardless of your commitment to Ben, you'll still keep on seeing Sophy!' she blurted bitterly.

There was a taut silence. Even the cicadas seemed to abruptly stop shrilling.

'No.' Marco's voice was suddenly flat and grim. 'That wasn't what I wanted to discuss, Polly.'

She caught her breath, hating herself now for letting her insecurities show so blatantly.

'Sorry...' She gave a short, mirthless laugh. 'Maybe that was rather...tactless of me? It's a bad habit of mine—attack as the best form of defence.'

'What are you defending yourself against? Your involvement with Paul?'

A bright light seemed to have begun dancing in front of her eyes, a painful haze of misery. She forced a stiff shrug.

'We both went into this marriage knowing we were probably...committed elsewhere,' she lied doggedly. The humiliation of her surrender to Marco earlier was eating at her inside, like acid on the armour of her pride.

'Speak for yourself. On the plane, I told you Sophy and I have never been lovers,' Marco reminded her acidly, toying with his wineglass. 'You really didn't believe a word I said, did you? You're convinced I was lying.'

'Some men do lie; it's more convenient than baring their soul and facing the consequences,' she challenged miserably. 'I suspect it's also a lot more fun for them...'

'To hell with this,' Marco grated roughly. 'You were right— we shouldn't talk. How did you put it earlier? We say horrible things and fall out? Let's go back to bed, Polly. That's our only way of communicating, isn't it?'

Fury almost blinded her. She swallowed hot tears and heard herself saying bitterly, 'Right. Sex is everything. What did Sophy really want just now? A detailed account of how our honeymoon is going so far? Did you tell her? Is that how the two of you get your kicks?'

Even through the blur of anger she registered that she'd gone too far. She had never seen Marco's face so ruthlessly furious. His eyes were black with rage.

'I don't believe this....' He stood up, bent over her, his hands on the table as he scanned her white face. 'You think I want to play-act the dutiful husband for our son's sake—' his drawl was savagely bleak and bitter '—but that in private I'm going to lie and cheat, with no limit to the depth of depravity I'd sink to? Even conducting an affair with my new sister-in-law while my wife welcomes me into her bed with such touching eagerness...?'

Polly stood up quickly, breathing hard.

'This is terrible...' she whispered shakily. 'I see now, quite clearly...this is never going to work. I won't let you do this to me...I won't let myself be destroyed by you...'

Marco reached out and took her wrist in a grip that bruised.

'Don't even think about leaving me, Polly,' he grated, a shudder in his voice.

'I can't stay with you...not like this... How can I ever trust you, when you're so obviously lying to me about Sophy?'

'If you go, Ben stays. Remember that. Just damn well remember that!'

'To grow up without his mother's love and support?' Her voice cracked bitterly. 'Is that supposed to be a preferable option, Marco?'

With a sob, she wrenched free and turned to run down the outside stairs, blindly following the path from the villa onto the dark cliff, searching for the path down to the beach.

It was pitch-dark; angrily dashing away the tears, she scanned the sky for a moon and couldn't find one. A moonspinners' night, she thought, remembering a childhood story. A night of blackness for hunted animals to move around in safety, while the moonspinners spun away the silver threads of moonlight to give cover of darkness.

She was feeling rather like a hunted animal herself. Marco was the hunter. He'd trapped her, and he wasn't about to let her go.

Finding the path, she stumbled downwards, hardly seeing where she was walking; the air smelled of salt and warm undergrowth, and it was still and hot, with hardly any breeze. The low bushes caught at her legs. When she stopped walking, the heat felt like a blanket wrapping itself around her. She could hear the sea, rhythmically hissing and breaking on the beach. The cicadas had gone quiet, surprisingly, but an owl still fluted somewhere in the darkness.

Polly drew a ragged breath, and almost tripped off the end of the path onto the soft, grainy sand. Her feet crunched as she made her way to the sea's edge. She stared at the dark expanse of water, stretching to the paler horizon.

Her heart ached for Ben, and home, and normality. She couldn't see how she could stand this artificial situation between herself and Marco. She'd go mad... Marco was obsessed, she decided, wiping away more tears with the back of her hand. He was obsessed with claiming his son, obsessed with creating the perfect family for Ben. Inconveniences like his relationship with Sophy, like her own feelings, were to be swept aside by his vision of a perfect world for his son. Her own unhappiness at this arrangement was to be her punishment for the unforgivable stain on the family honour of not telling him about Ben... The two most important things in Sicilian culture were family and honour, that was what Aunt Ruth had said. Those were the prime motivations for a Sicilian male.

Marco seemed to be in ruthless pursuit of little else right now. Today's seduction would have been a practical ploy—why spend his honeymoon in arguments and accusations, when he could enjoy a week of sexual satisfaction with a willing partner?

'Polly...?' His husky voice behind her shocked her into a muffled scream. She spun round in panic.

'Don't look at me like that,' he said grimly, reaching out to capture her by the shoulders, giving her a slight shake. 'What do you think I'm going to do to you? Strangle you and throw you to the sharks?'

'Leave me alone,' she whispered, struggling to free herself.

'No. Not like this. Come back up to the house.'

'No...'

'Come on, Polly...' There was rough desperation in his voice;

he took hold of her. 'You're...overwrought. I can't leave you here like this...'

'I just want some time alone. I need to think...'

'We're both tired,' he persisted firmly. 'I definitely need some sleep. I guess you feel the same. Come back to the house now.'

With gentle but determined pressure he was guiding her back towards the path. Every muscle in her body tensed with the indignity of being frogmarched back to the house. But suddenly she saw the futility of physically fighting him. He was taller, bigger, stronger, way out of her league when it came to pitting her strength. With a shudder of defeat she let him lead her back up to the lights of the villa, and into the bedroom.

It looked welcoming and cosy; the bedside lamps threw pools of warm golden light on the pine lockers and he'd straightened the bed.

Keeping her eyes averted from his face, she collected her nightdress and toiletries, and walked back to the door.

'Where the hell are you going?'

'Upstairs. I'll sleep on the sofa on the terrace...'

'You're mad. You'll be eaten alive by mosquitoes.'

'Then...I'll sleep in one of the armchairs inside,' she told him over her shoulder. He was standing in the middle of the room, watching her, hands thrust in the pockets of his jeans, his face dark and expressionless.

'There's no need for that.' There was a flat note of authority in his voice which made her hesitate slightly. 'You can have the bedroom. I'll go upstairs.'

She'd begun shaking her head. He crossed the room quickly, putting his hand on her shoulder.

'Polly, I know your opinion of me couldn't get a lot lower.' His voice was laced with dry sarcasm. 'But even a man like me wouldn't let his new wife sit up all night in an armchair.'

She glared at him, her heart thudding uncertainly.

'If you're offering to do it yourself, it can't be impossible!'

There was a moment's flaring silence; Marco's mouth twitched slightly in bleak amusement.

'It's not impossible; just not recommended. Give in, Polly.

You know you'd sleep better lying on a proper bed. And you look to me like someone in need of a good night's sleep.'

'You said a few minutes ago that you needed a good night's sleep yourself.'

'This,' Marco pronounced with heavy patience, 'is one of the stupidest conversations I've ever had. How about a compromise? We keep to our own sides of the bed and restrain our sexual urges?'

She felt herself going hot under the biting irony.

'How do I know I can trust you?'

'Now you're asking.' His eyes narrowed to dark blue slits. 'I could promise, on my honour?' he suggested silkily.

'On your *honour*? You're such an *honourable* man, aren't you? Don't make me laugh, Marco...'

Turning away, she was about to disappear into the bathroom, but he abruptly barred her way. Stopping in her tracks, her legs shaking, she risked a quick look at him. One glimpse of his haggard expression and her heart began to thud erratically.

'What are you doing...?'

'Acting in character...after one insult too many, my darling wife,' he grated raggedly; he pulled her resisting body against him and bent to kiss her with a heart-stopping skill which left her boneless in his arms. Then she was scooped up and laid, triumphantly, on the bed.

'Marco, let go of me...' she began, her heart thudding.

'Why should I? I'm claiming payment for that last bit of hypocrisy...' he teased softly. 'I'm damned if I'll let you get away with that...'

This time she did fight in earnest. She punched with her fists, until he captured her wrists in one strong hand and pinned her arms above her head. She kicked as hard as bare feet would allow, until he lowered his weight to trap her legs to the bed.

'Polly, stop it...stop fighting me, darling...' he breathed, his lips tracing irresistible trails of kisses down her temples, her jawline, her neck, finding the pulse-points above her collarbone and using his tongue to tease and arouse her until she gasped and wriggled, and finally subsided beneath him with a churning of panic and a stab of need.

Part of her, she recognised in distress, was a traitor, because that part—unbelievably—welcomed this physical closeness, which was sweet and familiar and the essence of her relationship with Marco. It was a poor second to emotional commitment, but if it was all Marco could give her it felt like crumbs to a beggar.

He was stroking her, gently but hungrily, as if she were the enemy he needed to subdue with sensuality; his fingers moved along the slender column of her throat, smoothing the hollows and then curving up over the swell of her breasts, pushing the thin straps of her dress away from her shoulders.

In a last-ditch attempt to save her self-esteem she tried to scramble up as he started to ease her dress off, but she didn't move fast enough. She was caught, her heart hammering in desire and shame, trapped in his arms, dragged back beneath his hardness and warmth.

'Take your hands off me,' she managed, in a strangled hiss.

'Do you really want me to?' With shaky intensity he was caressing her upper arms, easing the stretchy aqua fabric away from her breasts. She'd worn the dress braless, because of the tiny straps, and she felt the draught of air from the revolving fan cool on her exposed flesh. Hating her own weakness, she felt her skin shiver into tiny goosebumps as he stroked his knuckles over her softness, lingered on the growing peaks of her nipples...

'You promised! *Marco...!*' He'd bent to suckle at one tight, throbbing nipple, and she caught her breath on a moan of unbearable desire.

'No, I only said that I *could* promise.' Looking up at him, she registered that his eyes were dark with pain, as well as desire, and misery clutched at her stomach. 'Only a man of *honour* would keep his promise. Isn't that so, *cara mia...?*'

'Marco...' She gave a despairing sob. 'Sex won't solve any of our problems...'

'Maybe not...but it's good, right? Why deny it?' he murmured, plundering her mouth, kissing her neck, her ears, her temples, then her breasts, and her stomach, and her thighs, smoothing and coaxing her shivering body until the hot river of desire surged deep and treacherous inside her. 'If we talk we mess things up. So this is how we communicate, remember? We're allowed to do this, my darling, because this is the blessed state of matrimony, intended for the procreation of children...we're meant to be together, you and I, loving or hating—maybe it's the same thing...'

'No, Marco...it isn't...' she sobbed thickly. She was arching convulsively beneath his exploring fingers, willing herself not to respond but sinking into the hot darkness of passion and wanting and desire, feeling the urgency of her need for him rising up to topple all other emotions...

'Then maybe we'll settle for wanting, Polly... Say you want me...say it...'

'No...'

She was crying, tears of passion and emotion welling and blurring her eyes, a lump of bitter despair in her throat. Marco didn't love her. And she loved him. She couldn't cope with the betrayal and humiliation, knowing he was using her sexuality against her, exploiting her weakness for his own purposes, punishing her for everything...

She was fighting him for real now, blindly pushing him away. She felt a shudder go through him, felt his whole body tense against her violent struggles.

'Say it, Polly...'

'No, *no*...!' From somewhere she found the strength to reject him. The words were torn from her on a furious sob. 'Marco, I *don't* want you—not like this, not when I can't trust your commitment to me, even on our honeymoon.... Do you hear? Stop, stop it...let go of me...'

Suddenly, he let her go. She rolled off the bed and staggered to her feet, dragging up her dress to cover her breasts, trembling all over.

He slowly pushed himself up, and sat motionless on the edge of the bed; she stared at him, heart pounding, rooted to the spot.

He thrust unsteady hands through his hair, then stood up slowly and looked round almost blindly, his expression dazed and blank, his eyes still black with sexual hunger. He found his jeans and roughly pulled them on. He pulled his T-shirt over his head.

'For God's sake, get back into bed,' he said flatly, walking to the door. The blank, dazed look had faded. The expression in his eyes now held what looked like contempt, or disgust— whether for her or for himself Polly couldn't be certain. 'And don't look so terrified. I've got the message.'

'Where are you going?'

He glanced briefly back at her.

'I've got a date with some mosquitoes.'

CHAPTER NINE

WHEN Polly woke, the travel clock by her bed told her it was a quarter past ten. She lay for a while, not moving, her eyes on the ceiling. The fan still revolved, but more slowly; Marco must have looked in at some point and turned it down.

Marco. She turned her head slowly, focused on the bright stripes of sunlight filtering through the shutters. The details of last night came back to her, and then she did move, convulsively, curling onto her side beneath the tangle of the sheet, drawing her knees up to her chest and clutching her arms round herself.

She'd hardly slept; the effort of physically rejecting him had left her quivering with need, emotionally wound up, like a spring...

She stifled a small sob as waves of despair swept over her.

For Ben's sake she was entangled in this mess of a relationship, the most complex of messes she could ever imagine. But however much she fooled herself that she could stay aloof, yesterday had proved her wrong.

She sat up, saw her tousled reflection in the mirror opposite. Her blonde hair was wildly untidy, and she had panda smudges of tiredness under her eyes. With a heavy heart, she showered and dressed. It was hot; they'd probably go to the beach. She slipped on a brief turquoise sundress over a matching bikini. Dark glasses were essential, she decided, rummaging in her bag until she found them. Putting them firmly in place, she went out into the heat of the morning, and prepared to go in search of her husband.

She heard the ring of the mobile phone on her way up the steps. Marco, in white polo shirt and navy blue linen bermudas, was sitting at the table on the terrace, breakfast things scattered around him, speaking on the phone in rapid Italian.

He clicked the phone off as she joined him at the table.

'Good morning.' He eyed her expressionlessly, his tone softly drawling. 'I brought fresh croissants from the bakery in the village. Yours are keeping warm in the oven. I made fresh-ground coffee, too.'

'Thank you.'

'Any ideas about what you want to do today?'

She shrugged stiffly.

'No.'

'Okay. I thought we could swim and sunbathe. Then maybe we could go back over to Trapani for dinner tonight. There are some good fish restaurants around the port. We can go across in the hydrofoil early evening—we can still spend most of the day on the beach. How does that sound?'

Polly shrugged slightly. Marco's mood this morning seemed to be polite, distant, and wary. She felt on shifting, dangerous ground.

'Well...I suppose...fine.' She cleared her throat awkwardly. 'That sounds...fine.'

'Good.' He watched her steadily, his eyes unreadable.

She stood up again, intending to go and get her breakfast. He pushed her gently back into her seat.

'Stay there. I'll get your breakfast.' He paused, then lifted the dark glasses away from her eyes and studied her face for a few intent seconds. 'How are you this morning, Polly?'

'I'm fine,' she said quickly. 'Thanks for the lie-in...'

'The least I could do.'

'Really?' She swallowed, uncertain of her role in the face of this unfamiliar civility. 'How were the mosquitoes?'

'Surprisingly interested in my left foot. Luckily I had some antihistamine in the car...'

He let the sunglasses fall gently back onto her nose and disappeared into the kitchen, returning with a dish of croissants and a jug of hot coffee.

She took a croissant, spread it sparingly with butter and apricot jam.

There was a short silence. Marco poured coffee into both their cups, and then leaned back in his chair, watching her through lidded eyes. She felt herself going hot all over, and it was nothing to do with the sun.

'Marco, about last night—' she began.

'I apologise. It won't happen again,' he interrupted flatly.

She jerked her head in surprise. She met a look that chilled her heart with its shadowy bleakness.

'I was angry,' he explained shortly. 'That's a dangerous motive for wanting...sex. I guess I deserved the mosquitoes, Polly.'

'I know you were angry...' She put down her croissant and stared at him, her appetite suddenly waning. 'Was that...because I made that quip about honour?'

'What do you think?'

'I know it was.' She nodded, pushing her plate away. 'It was...a provocative thing to say...I'm sorry.'

'You're sorry? Does that mean you retract the accusation?'

'You mean, do I think you are an honourable man?' Polly lifted her chin to meet his eyes.

'If that's how you want to put it. Do you?'

There was a coolness in his voice. That was what this polite, distant act was all about this morning, she realised. He was detaching himself from her. Her throat tightened.

'If you mean, will I blithely overlook the things you do and simply accept everything you say...well, I'm trying, Marco, but...'

'You're trying?' The sarcasm was intense.

'Marco...' she began huskily, her emotions ragged.

'I was fooling myself that this could work,' he drawled coldly. 'We'll have to sort something out when we get back to Tuscany. Meanwhile, to avoid gossip by cutting short the honeymoon, let's make the best of what we've got, shall we?'

'What have we got, exactly?' She had to force the question out. Sort something out when they got back to Tuscany? She found that she hadn't the courage to ask him to spell out precisely what he meant by that. She took a sip of coffee and her hand shook so much she spilled it in the saucer as she put the cup back.

'Without trust, we've got a marriage made in hell,' he answered softly. His dark face was devoid of emotion. 'Maybe I was arrogant to visualise anything else.'

She paused in the act of biting her croissant, staring at him.

She fought back the urge to burst into tears. She had to be strong. For Ben's sake, if no one else's...

He stood up, his eyes hardening.

'Finish your breakfast, Polly. Then we'll go to the beach.'

She managed to drink the rest of the coffee, and finish her croissant, but in the space of their short conversation her world seemed to have crashed into oblivion and neither tasted remotely appetising any longer.

Trapani by night buzzed with life, with restaurants dotted all around the harbour. It was lively, noisy, and she was grateful for it. She suspected that Marco had picked tonight's venue deliberately. They could play-act the happy couple, with plenty to distract them from intimate conversation.

But the day had passed surprisingly quickly; they'd swum, sunbathed, lazed on the beach reading, and she'd collected handfuls of mother-of-pearl shells from a cove around the headland. Marco had the use of a motor launch in the bay and he'd taken her round the coast, showed her caves in the cliffs. She had to admit to herself that in spite of the cool reserve between them she'd enjoyed his company a lot—he seemed to share her love of history, so in place of anything contentious he'd entertained her with stories of the ancient Phoenicians, who'd made gruesome sacrifices to the gods; there'd been evidence unearthed on sites south of Trapani airport...

'You choose a place to eat,' he suggested coolly now, as they strolled slowly along the harbour-front. Hordes of relaxed Italians thronged the pavement, enjoying their habitual evening walk before dinner. 'Pick a restaurant you like the look of...'

'That's silly,' she protested, trying not to tense up as he took her hand and lightly linked her arm through his. 'You know this place. I don't...'

She briefly glimpsed their reflections in the smoked glass windows of a parked car, and registered with a pang that they looked like the perfect, jet-set couple: Marco in expensive dark trousers and designer shirt, herself in one of her new Italian outfits—a short, figure-hugging white Lycra dress which had turned a few men's heads as she walked.

'Okay.' Marco relented. 'We'll go to a favourite of mine. They do excellent lobster...'

'Marco! *Ciao*, Marco!' A man and a woman strolling towards them had stopped in delight, and greetings were exchanged in enthusiastic Italian. Polly watched kisses on either cheek between Marco and the woman, and hugs and slaps on the back between the two men. The couple were in their early thirties, both very dark, their faces aglow with pleasure at the unexpected meeting.

'My wife, Polly.' Marco was speaking in English, she realised, concentrating again on the conversation. 'Polly, this is Mario, an old friend and fellow lawyer, and his wife Giuliana.'

'*Piacere*, pleased to meet you,' Polly murmured, shaking hands and submitting with shy pleasure to the warm Latin kisses on either cheek.

'You speak Italian?' Giuliana asked, smiling. She wore a short black dress, very high heels and discreet gold jewellery, and she was slim and stunningly attractive, in typical dark Italian style.

'I'm afraid I don't—not to intelligent conversation standard yet, anyway.'

'No matter; we will speak in English. Marco has just told us that you are newly married! Congratulations, we are so pleased for you both!'

'You must eat with us,' Mario was insisting, switching to perfect English too as they turned towards a well-lit and busy restaurant on the harbour-front. 'This is a double celebration, Marco! Just married, and having achieved the most spectacular convictions this decade; how does it feel, Polly, to be the wife of the bravest lawyer in Italy?'

'What...?' Polly began curiously, as the head waiter effortlessly ushered them to the best table in the restaurant. 'What is he talking about, Marco?'

'Mario has a habit of exaggerating,' Marco said shortly. 'He's referring to a court case which finished last week. It's not important.'

Giuliana gave her a wry look as they faced each other over the table.

'You don't know?' She seemed nonplussed for a moment. 'Oh, but of course, you would have been preoccupied with wedding arrangements, perhaps...' She trailed off, evidently unable to convince herself that this was a likely cause of Polly's ignorance.

'Not everyone in Italy shares your loyalty to our home town in Sicily,' Marco said drily, 'and Polly has only recently arrived from England. She has no idea of our internal...vices and politics...'

'But surely—' Mario stopped, noting a warning glance from his wife. He abruptly switched the conversation to trivia—the coincidence of bumping into each other, news of mutual friends. They talked mainly in English, in deference to Polly, but she was conscious that they were skirting round the issue of burning interest to them all, and she felt belittled by Marco's refusal to explain.

Far too proud to beg him for an explanation in front of his friends, she concentrated instead on her meal. Marco had recommended the *cuscusu*, a local fish soup, and the lobster. It was delicious. When Mario and Marco occasionally lapsed into Italian and conversed with soft intensity, Polly pointedly ignored them and talked to Giuliana, who told her that she was a teacher.

'I long for a baby of my own,' Giuliana confided in Polly. 'Mario and I have been married four years, and I am thirty-two. I'm beginning to worry that time is ticking by, you know? Do you want children, Polly?'

There was a brief pause.

'Well...' Polly was hesitating, wondering what on earth to say, when she suddenly realised that Marco was listening.

'Polly already has a child. My son,' he said simply, his face deadpan. 'He is three.'

The Italian couple's reaction was so natural and congratulatory Polly began to like Mario and Giuliana very much indeed. She could be friends with these people, she decided privately, as the next few minutes were taken up with cautious explanations and an extremely expurgated version of how they'd been apart for so long and had been reconciled...

It wasn't until the end of the meal that the court case came up again. A silver trolley, containing a large chilled bottle of Krug and a cluster of tulip glasses, was wheeled with a flourish to their table. The restaurant-owner tapped on the table and made a small, flowery speech. He raised his glass to Marco's dedication and bravery in outwitting and bringing to justice in the courts on the mainland, in a series of masterly legal manoeuvres, a quantity of dangerous criminals from his home village on their island. He was their *angelo custode*, he added proudly. Their very own guardian angel...

Polly could feel her jaw dropping, and hastily closed her mouth. People at nearby tables turned and lifted their glasses to them. The evening was taking on a surreal aspect. Extracting themselves from the restaurant took at least twenty minutes. Only the need to catch the last hydrofoil to Favignana, and the fact that they were on their honeymoon, enabled them to escape, Polly reflected with shaky bewilderment.

Back at the ferry dock, she sat in silence beside Marco as they waited for the hydrofoil.

'Did I miss something in the Italian press?' she said at last.

'Possibly.' Marco stared straight ahead. The hydrofoil was approaching from the islands, skimming towards them in the darkness, lights dazzling on the water, with a drone like an aircraft.

'So what was all that about?'

'I told you, nothing important.'

'Those people wouldn't agree, obviously.'

'It was a case I've been working on for a long time. The outcome attracted a lot of publicity.'

'But why?' she persisted. 'Why are you so famous?'

Marco gave a short laugh. 'Famous? Some friends—one of whom is a fellow lawyer—congratulated me on a successful case, Polly. The restaurant-owner was probably put up to that little performance by Mario.'

'It didn't look like that to me. And the other people in the restaurant—they seemed to know all about it.'

He sighed abruptly. 'All right, you want a full account of my professional activities. As prosecuting counsel, I managed to persuade a particularly influential criminal that it would be in his interests to become a *pentito*...'

'A what?'

'To turn state's evidence—become a penitent.'

'You mean he gave information on people to reduce his own sentence?'

'Exactly.'

'So...?'

'So it resulted in some spectacular convictions.' Marco sounded drily amused. 'It dragged in a whole net-load of other criminals, some of whom were posing as upright and honest citizens while indulging in fraud and organised crime: a couple of politicians, some industrialists, even a magistrate or two. So the case made the headlines when it was all wrapped up. Some newspaper coined the nickname *angelo custode...*'

Polly was silent, staring at his profile. The hydrofoil had docked; passengers were disembarking. Along with the other people waiting, she and Marco both stood up.

'It sounds as if you've made quite a name for yourself,' she agreed softly, her heart thudding suddenly. 'Guardian angel? Was it...I mean, doesn't that put you in some kind of danger, Marco? You're not...you're not on someone's hit-list?'

'Not now,' he assured her quietly. 'And even before the convictions I was running no more risk than if I'd been doing the job of...say, a policeman, or a fireman. Why, are you worried about Ben? Do you think I've been irresponsible, claiming my son under the circumstances? I promise you that neither you nor Ben have ever been in any danger. The case was over before you came out for the christening, Polly...'

'Actually, I wasn't thinking about Ben, or about myself...' She felt her face going hot.

'Then what?' he probed ruthlessly. 'Don't tell me you're worried about *my* safety and welfare?'

'Do you think I'd be glad to see you dead?' she whispered hoarsely.

'It might solve your dilemma,' he taunted. 'Although perhaps at least now you will stop suspecting me of links with the criminal underworld? One Hamilton misconception can be laid to rest, maybe?'

She felt tears sting her eyes. Not trusting herself to speak, she stared out across the dark water.

The mobile shrilled and Marco answered it, first in Italian, then abruptly switching to English. Polly listened abstractedly at first, then she suddenly caught a glimpse of Marco's face. She went cold inside. Her misery changed to an active sense of dread.

People were boarding the hydrofoil now, but she and Marco didn't move; they stood immobilised on the quay as groups of people moved forward around them.

'What? What is it?' she demanded, when he put the phone away and turned to look at her. The expression in his eyes made her stomach clench in fear.

'Ben's in hospital in Florence; some kind of swimming accident, from what I can gather...'

'Swimming accident?' she repeated faintly. 'How? Where?' Blackness rose and receded; cold terror clutched her.

'He was with Sophy. It's not clear exactly what happened...'

'Marco, he's all right? He'll be all right?'

'Yes, of course, don't panic; but we have to get back straight away, darling...'

'Yes, of course... Poor Ben, he'll be really frightened, and upset. He'll be wanting me, he'll expect me to be there—he always does if he hurts himself. But he'll be too proud to cry, especially if I'm not there...' She was striving for normality while she felt hysteria rising inside.

'Polly, sweetheart...' She jerked her head to look at him, and she was appalled at the black anxiety she saw in his face. '*Cara*, at the moment Ben won't know that you're not there. My father...' Marco spoke gently, but his voice held a rough catch. 'My father says that he's unconscious. There's a risk that he could have lapsed into a coma.'

The events that followed seemed to Polly to lack reality; these things were happening to someone else. She was just a numb, detached observer. The frantic telephone calls to decide on the fastest way back to Tuscany. The torment of waiting for a flight after a hectic drive to the airport in Mario and Giuliana's car.

When their plane was finally ready for take-off, Giuliana hugged Polly, her brown eyes full of tears.

'Your son will be all right,' she said huskily. 'I will pray for you.'

'Let us know,' was all Mario said, crushing Marco to his chest. Polly saw, from her strangely detached perspective, that Marco's face was ashen beneath the darkness of his skin. Her own body felt bloodless, as if she were the walking dead.

The short flight seemed endless, the taxi ride through Florence to the hospital a nightmare; even the weather conspired against them as a sudden vicious summer storm flung hailstones as big as marbles to crash against the windscreen like missiles from the gods, and there were menacing fizzes of lightning in the sky. The taxi driver cursed continually in guttural Italian. In the back of the taxi, Polly huddled for comfort against Marco, and she felt his arms abruptly tighten around her, until she could feel the dull thud of his heart under her cheek.

The hospital. A heart-stopping walk through white corridors, through endless swing-doors. In an ante-room members of the Daretta family, together with Sophy, stood or sat, pale and frowning, or crying quietly. In the room beyond a small shape lay inert, in the centre of a bed designed for a large adult. Monitors and drips were attached to him, surrounding him, alien obstacles blocking the way when all Polly desired was space and freedom to get to him, to take him in her arms, to cradle and revive him, to breathe life and health back into him.

Regardless of medical staff, oblivious to the relatives, Polly reflected later that she might have killed anyone who stood in her way as she followed a magnetic path to her son and wrapped him in her arms, pressed her lips to his cheek. She said his name, over and over again, talked to him in a rush of nonsense she could never remember, as tears poured down her face unchecked.

Eyes closed, silky lashes curving on his white cheeks, Ben slept on.

A long time elapsed before she looked up and saw Marco. His eyes were black, his face white with strain. He took one of Ben's small hands as she watched, spoke to him in husky Italian. He looked up and met her eyes, and she recognised the glitter of emotion there because it so accurately mirrored her own.

She snatched a frayed breath, then, and controlled her tears. Whatever she and Marco lacked, they shared a powerful thing in their love for Ben.

'Come and talk to the doctor,' he said quietly. He was tenderly laying Ben's tiny hand back on the sheet. She had to avert her eyes quickly to stay calm enough to walk away.

'I found him floating face down in the water,' Sophy said, in a tight, expressionless voice.

'You found him?' Marco's voice held a note of controlled coldness which made Polly turn to stare at him. 'What do you mean, exactly? Weren't you with him?'

'Of course I was with him. I just...turned away for a few seconds, that's all...!'

They'd had a long conversation with the doctor about Ben's chances of a full recovery. The doctor, steeled to stay cool and professional in the face of raw grief and anger, had been resolutely factual. The prognosis seemed to be uncertain at this stage. If Ben came round in the next few hours, the danger would be lessened. But there was no guarantee that he would do so. If he lapsed into a coma, the question of brain damage would be a key factor. There was no way of knowing, especially in so small a child, how much damage could already have occurred; it all depended on how long he'd been without oxygen.

Now, still feeling numb and dislocated, like a figment of some ghastly nightmare, Polly was sitting in the small ante-room, shivering slightly in the same skimpy white dress she'd worn a hundred or so years ago in Trapani to dine out with Marco. Sitting in a semi-circle around her were Marco, Ruth, Tino and Sophy, plastic cups of coffee in front of them, while Sophy tried to explain what had happened.

She'd apparently offered to look after Ben while Ruth and Tino went shopping and Marietta was feeding the twins. Ben had suddenly announced that he wanted to go and practise his new swimming technique. Seeing no harm in it, Sophy had driven him to Marco's farmhouse, and it was there that the accident had happened.

'So you turned away for a few seconds, and in that few seconds my infant son runs up to the swimming pool, slips and hits his head, knocking himself unconscious, falls into the water and floats face down for an unconfirmed length of time?'

Polly caught her breath, put a warning hand over Marco's. Sophy had gone very pale. She looked genuinely upset; the chalk-white of her face beneath her upswept golden hair made her look like a doll.

Polly glanced up at Ruth and Tino. They were tense-faced, but they were looking at Marco, and seemed unwilling to intervene. She was in torment herself, but Marco, though outwardly calm, seemed to be grimly fending off a violent breakdown.

'Let's save our energy for Ben,' she whispered shakily. 'Blaming Sophy isn't going to help. I'm sure she feels bad enough as it is, Marco...'

He ignored her, his eyes on Sophy.

'Do you, Sophy?' he went on, with ominous softness.

Polly glanced at him again, her heart jolting. She was beginning to suspect that he'd already talked to Tino or Ruth, and knew something that she didn't...

Sophy retorted defensively, 'Of course I feel bad! I offered to entertain him for the afternoon, and I was only talking to Luciano for a few minutes...'

'Talking to Luciano? He was there with you?'

'Well, no, but...'

'You mean you talked to him on the phone? You had a mobile with you?'

'Well, no...' Sophy's colour had risen slightly.

'You went to the house to use the phone? The house is five minutes' walk from the swimming pool. How could you leave a three-year-old by deep water, unsupervised?'

'You're just jealous because I was phoning Luciano!'

There was a silence like a blanket of ice, descending on the whole group.

'I have always thought of you as a friend.' Marco spoke with a fiercely cold precision; suddenly, he was all Sicilian, no hint of the English reserve that was an equal part of his character. 'I only recently discovered my mistake. I found out that you don't know how to be a friend, Sophy.'

'Marco...'

'My friends wouldn't sabotage my relationships,' he went on ruthlessly. 'They wouldn't tell blatant lies to stop me getting together with the mother of my child. They wouldn't cause trouble on my wedding day. They wouldn't ring my mobile number hoping to wreck my wedding night. Most of all, they wouldn't neglect my son's safety by talking on the phone when they should have been watching him. I'd say our friendship is over, Sophy. Wouldn't you?'

Sophy jumped to her feet, her face bright red with fury and humiliation, and turned to run from the room. On shaky legs, Polly dashed after her. She caught up with her halfway down one of the endless white corridors.

'Wait! Sophy, wait...'

Her stepsister stopped and spun round, her face mask-like.

'Go back to your beloved Marco, Polly,' she advised mockingly. 'You've obviously won; good luck to you!'

'Don't go like this,' Polly pleaded, dashing away tears. 'Not thinking that we blame you for what happened... Marco doesn't mean it; he's just...he's just broken up over Ben—he's known him such a short time and...he's just so afraid...so terrified that...' She couldn't bring herself to put into words the unthinkable. She couldn't even bear to contemplate it, however fleetingly...

Sophy didn't move. But her face crumpled slightly.

'I'm sorry,' she muttered. She sounded awkward, as if these were the most difficult words she'd ever said.

There was a heavy pause following this. A nurse walked briskly past them, then a young doctor, his white coat flapping, consulting notes as he walked.

Sophy had started to cry. Polly went to put her arms round her. She felt a shudder go through her sister's body as she hugged her. Sophy stiffened, then began to talk quickly, shakily.

'I suppose.... Oh, hell, Polly, I do feel guilty about Ben; it was just an accident, but I probably should have been keeping a closer eye on him, and if anything happens to him— Oh, God, Polly...he will be all right, won't he? Say he's going to be all right...'

'You made a mistake, Sophy,' Polly managed, while her stomach contracted in fierce anguish at the vision of Ben, only three and a half, being left to play, unsupervised, around a swimming pool. 'You're not used to young children. Torturing yourself won't undo what happened. Try not to blame yourself too much...'

'*So* sweet-natured and forgiving. That's half your problem. If things were the other way round, I'd never forgive *you*! I've been the biggest bitch, I suppose...' There was a brief pause. They both stiffened slightly, and as Sophy stepped back she took a deep breath, then a stream of words came tumbling out. 'Marco's right, I...I have lied. To him, and to you. He and I have only ever been friends—his choice, not mine. I wanted us to be lovers and he didn't, but he kept in touch and encouraged the friendship because of the family, not wanting to keep the feud going into the next generation, as he put it, and...and I couldn't stand it when I realised he had a thing for you! I just couldn't face the idea...'

Sophy was searching Polly's white face. There was such guilt in her expression Polly knew for certain that Sophy, for once, was telling the truth.

'So all these years you've been making it up? About you and Marco being lovers?'

'You catch on fast,' Sophy quipped bitterly, dashing another tear away. 'Yes, that's what I'm saying. Because *I* wanted him! Do you understand...?'

'I...suppose I understand...' She heard herself say the words. But did she? She could understand the desperate futility of wanting someone who didn't appear to want you. But she had difficulty in understanding how Sophy could have lied and lied, and in doing so cause so much damage, all these years...

'I even took some letters he wrote to you,' Sophy blurted, half defiantly, completing her confessional. 'While you were in America with Paul I came home to Hamilton Priory. I saw these letters addressed to you lying on the hall table, Marco's handwriting on the envelopes. I...I hid them...'

'Oh, Sophy...' Suddenly Polly was too drained to continue. She lifted a hand to touch Sophy's shoulder, then dropped it to her side.

'I know I've been awful.' Sophy sounded like a small child, desperate to be told she wasn't all bad. 'I'm probably being punished by the gods, or something—if anything happens to Ben, I don't know how I'm going to live with myself...'

'Sophy...what happened with Ben wasn't deliberate; I know that. Whatever you've done I do know you'd never do anything on purpose to hurt Ben...it was...non-attention—a moment's aberration on your part,' Polly said slowly. 'But interfering between Marco and me...' Fatigue and the stirrings of fresh, deep anger, made her sway slightly where she stood. 'Why, Sophy? Why have you always hated me so much?'

Her sister's face had gone paler. With a stiff movement, a defensive hunch of her shoulders, she said flatly, 'I was jealous.'

'Of me?' Polly shook her head. 'But why...?'

'You had all Dad's love, I suppose.' She shrugged. 'My dad ran off before my parents divorced. He never bothered to find out how I was. And when my mother married your dad, all I ever heard from him was, "Polly this...Polly that". You were the clever one, going to university, I was the stupid one, trying to be a model...and then Marco was the final straw...' Sophy's laugh had a hollow ring.

Polly drew a deep breath. She forced herself to speak.

'Sophy, come back with me. You don't have to leave. Marco will calm down...'

'No, it's better if I go. I'll give Luciano a ring. Tell him I need a shoulder to cry on,' Sophy said, with a flash of her usual insouciance, as if by confessing all to Polly she'd already freed her conscience. 'Or someone to buy me dinner, anyway. I might stay over at his place tonight; best if I keep out of the family circle, eh? I'll...I'll ring tomorrow, see how Ben is...'

With her feelings in chaos, Polly watched her sister walk quickly away, then disappear from sight round a corner.

Hurrying back to Ben's room, she met Ruth. The older woman was in tears, agitatedly looking left and right as if searching for someone, just outside the ante-room door.

Polly was to look back on that split second, paralysed where she stood in the hospital corridor. The unthinkable had happened. The agony was like nothing she'd ever encountered, like shrinking from the edge of an unimaginable pit of darkness and grief...

'Polly!' Ruth swooped on her, grasped her arms, her eyes red from weeping. 'Oh, my darling, I've been looking for you... The most marvellous thing—Ben's awake! He's awake!'

Marco burst out of the room at the precise moment that the world went black and Polly fainted.

CHAPTER TEN

'POLLY? Are you all right?' Marco's voice. She was in his arms, her head on his shoulder. Struggling back to awareness, she tried to leap to her feet.

'Ben—I have to see him...' she began, then stopped and clapped her hand to her mouth as a wave of sickness came over her.

'Polly...'

'Bathroom...' She was whisked into the adjoining bathroom and ignominiously, with Marco holding her tightly and supporting her head, she parted company with the contents of her stomach. Exhausted, she clutched the basin, ran the cold tap, splashed her face, rinsed her mouth.

'I must see Ben,' she said, her voice trembling. 'I don't know what made me faint like that, throw up like that. I'm so happy I could fly, and here I am doing this...'

'Shock,' Marco said gently, but matter-of-factly, helping her out of the bathroom, his arm very strong and reassuring as he led her into the inner room.

Ben lay in the hospital bed, his eyes still closed, like a tiny olive-skinned doll, tubes and monitors still attached, looking just the same as he'd looked a short while ago when she'd held him in her arms and he'd made no response. Ruth and Tino sat at one side, their arms round each other, watching him lovingly. Polly whirled round to search Marco's face, her heart clenching.

'Marco...?'

She felt his arm tighten.

'It's all right, darling. He only woke up for a few moments. But he's going to recover. The doctors say he's a tough little boy. They think he's going to be fine...'

Finding her strength at last, she went to take her son's tiny hand, and then to lay her cheek against his, to wrap him tenderly

169

in her arms. Her heart swelled as she felt a tremor of response, and then a small voice whispered 'Mummy...'

Angelina found her true vocation when Ben came home to the farmhouse. Content until this point in her life to be a mere housekeeper, now it seemed she was in her element as Ben's devoted carer, poised to attend to his every whim, jealous in her role of nurse and nanny.

'I have to be careful of her feelings,' Polly told Marco lightly, as they sat with pre-dinner martinis one evening. 'I was about to take Ben a mug of orange juice in bed a few minutes ago; I found myself asking her if she minded!'

'If she's getting too possessive, I'll say something.'

'Certainly not. I was joking; I think it's sweet that Ben's made such a conquest.'

'He'll make dozens when he's older,' Marco said.

'Like his father,' Polly said, without thinking.

There was a silence. She risked a glance at Marco, where he sat a few feet away. He looked relaxed, in denim jeans and striped navy and white overshirt, but there was a wary tension in his face which had been there ever since Ben's accident; no, since before that, since their bitter row at the villa in Favignana.

Since they'd been back at the farmhouse they'd kept to their own rooms; when they'd brought Ben home yesterday, he'd returned to his bed beside Polly's, just as before. It was as if their married state had never been.

They were sitting on the terrace beneath the wisteria. The evening light was beginning to fade. Angelina, her nursing duties fulfilled, was clattering happily in the kitchen, concocting dinner.

'Ben's accident seems unreal now,' Polly said, sipping her drink slowly. 'Some sticking plaster on his forehead is all he has to show for it.'

'He's tough,' Marco agreed. 'He's a Daretta.'

'He's half-Daretta, Marco, and half-Hamilton.'

Another uncomfortable silence stretched out between them. Polly put her glass down with an unsteady clink on the table and turned to look at Marco.

'You've inherited a lot from the English side of your family,' she said quietly.

His glance was unreadable.

'What's that supposed to mean?'

'All this Anglo-Saxon sang-froid.' She smiled slightly. Her heart was bumping painfully against her ribs as she gathered the courage to go on. 'Maybe we need to have a very Latin blazing row to clear the air...'

'Clear the air?' The cynical note in his voice made her heart shrink slightly. 'Is that all you think we have to do, Polly?'

She swallowed on a suddenly dry throat.

'We need to do something. This...tiptoeing around each other is tearing me apart, Marco. You're blocking me out. You're acting like a stranger. You're...you're polite, and civil...but the only time I've seen you smile is at Ben...'

Marco's gaze was a dark, lambent blue as he turned to stare at her.

'What did you expect?' he said. There was quiet bitterness in his voice. 'That I'd fall to my knees in gratitude just because Sophy told you the truth and you finally believed me, trusted me?'

She met his eyes in painful silence.

'Marco...' she began huskily, biting back tears. 'I'm sorry I didn't trust you. I'm so sorry. That's all I can say.'

'I know.'

'And that's not enough?' She already knew the answer. She gripped her hands tightly between her knees and found a point in the distance to fix her eyes on: a red pantiled roof in the distance between two dark Lombardy poplars.

He said flatly, 'I've been doing some thinking. I need some time alone.'

'Alone?' She echoed the word as if he'd told her he needed arsenic. 'Now just a minute.' She swung round on him, pain and anger engulfing her. 'You're the one who bulldozed us both into this marriage—you're the one who demanded total commitment from me just because I was the mother of your son, who kept my passport in case I escaped back to England, who insisted on a sexual relationship when I wanted things to stay platonic...'

'Polly, I need space.' He stood up, his mouth a grim line in a dark, shuttered face. 'I need time to sort out how I feel...'

'How *you* feel? How do you think *I* feel?'

'At a guess, I'd say trapped—manipulated into a marriage with someone you don't love. I need to work out how I feel about being married to a woman who has this much respect—' he measured half an inch between thumb and forefinger with an angry jerk '—for my integrity.'

Polly stood up now, her knees feeling shaky.

'Marco, just a minute...'

'On our "honeymoon", you made accusations I still can't forgive. You scorned my word, showed contempt for my morals, were prepared to believe the worst possible motives for every move I made...'

'And even though I've said I'm sorry, you're going to bear a grudge?' she flung at him, in a choked whisper. 'Maybe there's far more Sicilian than Anglo-Saxon blood in your veins, Marco.'

'Maybe there is.'

They faced each other across what seemed like a widening barrier of bitterness. Polly hugged her arms round her chest, trying to ward off the fear of imminent breakdown. She had to stay strong; she had her pride, if very little else. But inside she was dying...

'So what are you suggesting?' She meant it to come out as a forceful enquiry, but it was a hoarse whisper.

'I've got business in Rome. I'll be away for two, maybe three weeks...'

She sucked in her breath.

'In that case, I want my passport, Marco. In ten days or so Ben should be able to travel. I need to go home to England for a while. With Ben.'

She lifted her chin at the dark flare of anger in his eyes, and held his gaze with all the courage she could find.

'So you can see *Paul*?'

'Whatever you want to believe,' she said bitterly.

He stared at her for a long time.

He said at last, 'Tell Angelina I'm eating out, would you?'

And he turned and left her.

*   *   *

'Mummy? You've got dust all over your face. Is that why you're crying?'

Polly sat cross-legged, three weeks later, on the attic floor at the top of Hamilton Priory. She jerked her head up at Ben's innocent enquiry. He was plundering the dressing-up trunk, containing costumes the Hamiltons had accumulated over the years, mainly for Christmas family charades. He was wearing a Napoleon Bonaparte hat at a rakish angle which hid one eye, a moth-eaten fox-fur stole and a plastic sword buckled round his waist.

She was reading Marco's letters. She was still reeling from the shock and surprise of finding them. It had been pure chance; Sophy had sworn, defensively, that she'd forgotten where she put them.

A rainy spell this afternoon had made her think of bringing Ben up here; there were old toys from her own childhood—books and board games stacked on shelves, a rocking horse, and the precious dressing-up trunk. Ben, delving in amongst the piles of clothes and hats, had found the letters, given them an uninterested glance, and, while he searched for more exciting treasures, had dropped them absently on the floor at Polly's feet.

'No, sweetheart, it's not the dust,' she said, dashing a hand across her cheek to stop the tears. 'I'm reading something sad. That's all...'

'A story?'

'Um...no, darling, not exactly...' Not a story, she reflected, swallowing hard, but an intense insight into Marco's feelings, almost too painful to read, written the day after their meeting in Cambridge...

He'd really cared. After they'd made love, he'd felt that she was 'too important to lose', he'd written in bold black ink on cream vellum writing paper, and he hoped she felt the same way. He was sorry for ranting and lecturing—he'd just felt so bad about losing control like that, making love to her while she was still groggy. But he desperately wanted to see her, he'd written, talk to her...

Believe it or not, I love you, Polly. I think it started in Prizzi. You were so sweet and earnest, but I kept thinking of you as my little cousin, not grown up yet. But last night made me realise I've wasted too much time...

With her eyes blurred with tears, she kept going back to those unbelievable words. 'I love you, Polly...' All this time these letters had lain here, having been read by Sophy and hidden. The extent of her stepsister's malicious damage made her head spin.

She folded the letter with trembling fingers, delved in the pocket of her shorts for a tissue and blew her nose. Marco had written from the heart, taken a risk, made himself vulnerable. What must he have thought when she made no response? She could hardly bear to contemplate the blow to his pride. If she'd ever come close to really hating Sophy, it was now, as the full impact of her meddling became clearer. Sophy had loved Marco herself; that had been her excuse. But if she'd hidden these letters she couldn't have loved him. If you loved someone, you surely couldn't cause them the pain that Marco must have suffered, baring his soul like this, thinking he was being ignored...

Polly gulped back more tears. All this time, while she had been secretly loving Marco, Marco had loved her in return. All these wasted years he could have been there for her, there for Ben...

There were two more letters. The second had been written a week later, saying that as he hadn't heard from her he'd been about to write to her direct, in America, at the address her father had given him, until he'd heard from Sophy that she'd gone there for the whole summer with her long-term boyfriend, Paul. The third, written two weeks after that, was heartbreakingly short and cool, stating that if there were any repercussions from their one act of lovemaking, she knew where to find him, and that he'd always be there if she needed him...

'If it's not a story, what is it?' Ben was watching her with growing curiosity.

'It's...it's some letters from your daddy...'

'Why are they sad?'

'Because I didn't know he'd written them...' Polly got herself under control with an effort and stood up, stuffing the letters into her pocket.

'How did they get in the dressing-up box?'

'That's a bit complicated, darling...'

'When is Daddy coming?' Ben drew the sword from his belt and began thwacking the dressing-up chest, showing an alarming capacity for martial violence. 'On the phone he said he would come and see me soon. I want my daddy to come. I love my daddy.'

'I love your daddy too,' Polly agreed huskily as they went down the bare staircase to the top landing, and onto the red-carpeted floor which led to the sweeping stairs down to the hall.

The deep voice talking to Mary in the hall made her jump as if she'd been shot.

Darting to the banisters, she saw Marco standing in the hall at the foot of the stairs, tall and lean and dark, in jeans and white polo-shirt, with Mary hovering in the background, smiling uncertainly.

'Marco!'

'Daddy!'

Polly grabbed Ben's hand to stop him from rushing headlong down the stairs, and together they went slowly to greet him.

Marco bent and swung Ben into his arms, hugged him and kissed him on each cheek, and solemnly admired his outfit. Then, as Ben chattered non-stop about his day's activities, Marco held out his hand to Polly. Her heart missing beats wildly, she put her hand into his and looked searchingly into his eyes.

'How are you?' he said softly. 'Apart from disguising yourself as a chimney sweep?'

'Missing you.' She wiped the back of her hand over her eyes again, and looked at the dusty streaks with a choked laugh. 'How about you?'

Marco's voice was husky. 'Missing you.'

'Daddy, you're not listening...!'

'Sorry, Ben...' Marco hoisted Ben's wriggling body high into the air and grinned up at him. 'Not listening is the worst crime,' he admitted humbly, lowering him to the Turkish-carpeted floor. 'Alongside not trusting, not believing, and not forgiving...'

Polly thought her blood would explode in her veins, the rush of heat and emotion was so intense.

'Ben...' She eased the fox-fur stole off her son's shoulders, in case he overheated in all the excitement, and bent down to look into his eyes. 'Darling, Mummy and Daddy have lots to talk about; can you help Mary with dinner for a little while?'

'That's right, my lovely,' Mary said coaxingly, holding out her hand. 'Pip and Davy are coming round soon; you can make dough models with them if you like?' Pip and Davy were two of Mary's horde of little nephews and nieces, who'd provided instant playmates for Ben on many occasions.

Ben put his thumb in his mouth. 'Is Daddy going away again?'

Polly glanced up at Marco, her heart contracting. His dark eyes held an intense, shadowy question; she looked back at Ben and quickly shook her head.

'No,' she told Ben, her eyes glistening with tears, 'I don't think Daddy's going away again.'

'Ben looks well,' Marco said.

'Yes. He's been running wild on the beach and in the sea with Mary's little nephews.'

'He hasn't been put off the water, then?'

'Far from it.' After their initial unguarded pleasure at seeing each other, they were conversing with awkward politeness—like a couple of strangers, she reflected, with a pang of anxiety. Marco seemed to be keeping his distance from her.

'I've considered putting him on a long lead recently. His sense of adventure seems to be developing along with his swimming skills.' She smiled slightly. 'I'm trying not to be over-protective, but it's hard.'

Having washed the dust and streaks from her face and hands, she ushered Marco through stone-flagged passageways to the small back sitting room overlooking the sloping rear lawns. It was a square, cosy room, with deep pink walls, dozens of oval-framed pictures and a green-grey carpet on polished oak boards. She turned to look at him as she closed the door. She waved a hand with polite nervousness to the antique chaise longue beneath the stone-mullioned window.

'I haven't been in this house for ten years,' he murmured wryly. 'Not since old Grandma Hamilton tossed her well-chosen insults at me.'

Her heart jerked in her chest.

'Don't, Marco...' she said tautly. 'Don't bring up the past again...'

'Don't worry, I'm not going to. It just feels strange, that's all. Polly, come and sit down.' He sat at one end of the chaise longue, stretching his denim-clad legs out in front of him and crossing his arms over his chest. His face was wary, his eyes dark and unreadable.

Panic swept over her. He was going to call it all off. He'd implied this when they were in Favignana. They'd have to sort something out, he'd said. Pain grew like a hard lump in her stomach; she wouldn't let him walk away from her. Not through some twisted misunderstanding caused by someone else...

'I've kept myself busy while you've been away,' she said determinedly, hovering just in front of him, clasping her hands in front of her. 'Mary's been helping a lot with Ben, and I've been sorting out "The Family Tree"—I think, with the right computer back-up, I could probably try running it from Tuscany...'

'That's good. Polly—'

'And Janie has said she'll cover the English end. We can use e-mail to stay in contact. There's no reason why it shouldn't work...'

'No reason at all. I'm glad. That's great news.' His dark gaze held a gleam she couldn't decipher. 'Polly, I'd love to discuss your career plans, but can we do that later? Can we talk about us?'

Polly caught her breath. She felt unbearably agitated. She was still in her grubby T-shirt and shorts, her hair bundled anyhow into a ponytail. She felt totally unprepared for a heated discussion on how to rescue her five-week-old marriage.

She realised that he was holding out his hand to her. Swallowing hard, she put her hand in his. He closed his fingers over hers and tugged her down to sit beside him.

Now that she had hold of Marco's hand, her fingers clung to his, desperate to keep the physical contact.

'Darling...the way you're talking...' he began huskily. 'You were so sure we'd get our marriage back together?'

Her heart lurched. He tightened his hand around hers.

'Yes,' she said defiantly. 'Shouldn't I have been?'

He closed his eyes and expelled a sharp breath.

'I don't deserve you, sweetheart,' he said hoarsely. 'Will you forgive me?'

She stared at him, daring to look at him properly for the first time since he'd arrived and drinking in the sight of him as if it had been three years not three weeks since she'd seen him; there were fatigue lines around his eyes and mouth, his black hair was tousled from much hand-raking, and his gaze was hunted as he searched her face. She saw such intense, violent emotion in the blue-black depths that she felt her heart swell with love and longing for him.

'What for, exactly?'

'For behaving like an immature, self-obsessed bastard; for disappearing off to Rome; for walking out on you like that.'

She dropped her eyes to their linked hands.

She said quietly, 'I won't deny it hurt. Why did you have to go away?'

'Because I couldn't think straight,' he confessed heavily. 'Even though you told me what Sophy had said, I couldn't take it in. I'd grown used to thinking the worst—that you'd just ignored my efforts to get in touch after Cambridge, that you were in love with some fellow student called Paul, that you'd kept Ben from me because you didn't want to know me...' He stopped, breathing fast, his eyes shadowed. 'Forgive me? I'm so sorry, darling, for deserting you just when you and Ben needed support...'

'Yes, I forgive you. But only if you've come back to stay.'

'There's another question I need a straight answer to,' he followed up, his voice hoarse. 'Do you love me, Polly?'

She caught her breath. Looking up, she met his intense gaze.

'Of course I do,' she said simply, and then held his eyes, and waited in silence. 'Now it's your turn,' she prompted huskily. Her heart thudded violently against her breastbone.

'Polly, *cara*...' The look in his eyes was mesmerising. There was a catch in his voice when he went on, 'You must know how I feel about you... I've loved you for so long I can't remember not loving you. I want to be with you all the time. I can't believe I've made such a complete mess of things...'

'Are you mad?' she burst out. 'Asking for my forgiveness, when most of it's been *my* fault! Or Sophy's! All these years, and I never knew about these...' She fumbled in the pocket of her white shorts, and with shaking fingers produced the crumpled letters. 'All I had to go on was your horrified reaction that time in Cambridge...'

'I was horrified with myself because I'd betrayed a trust—you were a virgin, and worse still you were in no state to know what you wanted that day, Polly...'

'And then I went on thinking you were Sophy's, feeling that to foist my pregnancy on you would be the most selfish thing in the world...'

There was a brief pause.

'What about Paul? Why go to America with him?'

'He was...*is* just a friend...' She stifled a short, guilty laugh. 'That trip had been booked months before the Ball at Cambridge. The truth about Paul is...well, Paul's sexual persuasions lie in the other direction,' she said, blushing at the narrowing of Marco's eyes.

'He's gay?' Marco stared at her incredulously, then he shook his head. 'All these years I've been jealous of your relationship with a gay friend? *Dio.* Sophy told me you and Paul were seriously involved...' He gave a twisted smile, then a short laugh which held an edge of triumph. 'She claimed you'd gone to America as lovers...'

'Nothing Sophy said surprises me any longer.' Her face felt even redder.

'But you didn't rush to clarify the situation, Polly?'

'Sorry...' she met his eyes guiltily. 'I...I know I recently let you jump to other conclusions, but only because I wanted a defence; I didn't want you finding out how much I care about you. I love you so much, Marco. I couldn't handle the humiliation of your knowing if you didn't feel the same...'

Marco gazed at her, his eyes very bright.

'We're both in a position of equal strength, then,' he said softly, lifting her hand to his lips with infinite tenderness. 'You do know how much I love you?'

'I think so...' She caught her breath. 'Reading your letters helped...'

'Your local postal service isn't too hot. I'm sure I used first-class stamps.'

She nodded, laughing shakily. 'I suspect divine intervention. Ben found them in the dressing-up box in the attic. He dropped them at my feet as he was extracting his Napoleon hat from the jumble.'

Marco looked disbelieving. 'Sophy didn't admit where she'd put them?'

'Nope. She said she'd forgotten.'

He was silent for a few moments. His dark features twisted wryly. 'Divine intervention indeed. Though I'm not sure I relish you reading my love-sick outpourings of four years ago...'

'Are you saying you feel differently now?'

He slowly nodded, then cupped her face in his hands as her eyes flew wider.

'I know you better now. I have deeper feelings for you.'

'I was reading your letters just before you arrived,' she whispered, half-laughing, half-crying. 'You really cared when I ran out on you that day; you really wanted to see me again. You said making love to me meant something special and you hoped I felt the same way... Oh, Marco, of course I felt the same way— probably more so, you idiot. I've loved you since I was thirteen...'

There was a short silence. Then Marco groaned, and folded her into his arms.

'You'll never catch me admitting that the feeling was mutual at that stage,' he said in a muffled voice, against the top of her head. 'I thought you were cute when you were thirteen, but if I'd lusted after you then, I'd have needed locking up, sweetheart. I've loved you since you came to Prizzi, with Sophy...'

'And what was wrong with me at thirteen?'

There was a shake of laughter as he held her closer.

'Braces, plaits...'

She twisted her face up, intending to remonstrate, and he kissed her; it was a long, hard, hungry kiss that precluded conversation, triggering longings and needs which threatened to overwhelm them both.

'I know we've spoken on the phone when you've rung Ben,' she whispered, as they broke apart for air, 'but I feel like we've been apart for months not weeks, Marco; I've been going crazy...'

'Me too,' he said hoarsely, circling her waist with his hands and caressing the slight curve of her stomach above her shorts. 'Darling, Polly...I'm sorry. It was pride. I was trying to forget the things you said to me when we were arguing. Thinking you only married me because Ben needed his father. It was something Luciano said, in the end. Sophy had apparently told him that you loved me...'

'Sophy did?' Polly blinked, a slight smile lifting her mouth. 'Well, if she's done something to try and put things right, maybe she's not all bad.'

'Her chance of redemption?' Marco grinned, his eyes brilliant with feeling. 'Maybe. Polly, you do love me?'

'Utterly. Why do you think I married you?' She blinked at him, dazzled with happiness. 'You do love *me*?'

'Totally.'

She pulled his head down then, rumpling her fingers into his black hair, and kissed him with such sweet passion and surrender that he scooped her onto his lap and continued kissing her, his hands seeking the bareness of her midriff and exploring upwards with escalating desire until she gave a small, tremulous gasp and drew back slightly, hot and breathless.

'I've wanted you so much...'

'*Cara*, not a fraction as much as I've wanted you...'

'Oh, Marco....' She was already tugging the polo-shirt up to make contact with the rough warmth of his body, her senses swimming. 'Make love to me darling... I need you to...'

He glanced at the door, extricated himself from her for a few seconds and went to turn the key in the lock. Then he was across the room in two strides and she was in his arms.

'I'll never stay away from you this long again,' he breathed, with a shudder of passion. He was inhaling the scent of her skin as he pulled the T-shirt over her head, his mouth at the hollow of her neck as he stripped off her shorts. He unfastened her white lace bra and gazed at her breasts as if he'd never seen her naked before.

'You're so gorgeous,' he said hoarsely. 'More gorgeous than ever...' He dropped his eyes to the slimness of her ribcage and ran his fingers over her ribs. 'Even if you do need to put on a bit of weight...'

'*Marco!*' Half-laughing, half-indignant, she felt herself blushing.

'Sorry...but you're looking thinner, darling. I'll worry about you if you get too thin...' He buried his face against the softness of her breasts, and she gasped as his teeth grazed the sensitive tips.

'I haven't had much appetite these last few weeks. Maybe I've just been pining for you. Anyway, maybe that's just your Italian blood...' she teased, shivering as he picked her up and laid her on the chaise longue, pausing only to discard his own clothes, revealing the dark, hard, muscled body she adored before coming down beside her with swift possessiveness. 'Maybe you like your women rounded and voluptuous?'

'I like my women exactly like you,' he assured her, sliding her panties over her hips and kissing her soft stomach. Polly caught her breath, remembering something, astonished at herself for not remembering before. He sensed her sudden tension and he stopped.

'What? Are you all right, sweetheart?'

'Yes...yes!' She was laughing slightly, biting her lip with rueful embarrassment. 'Oh, Marco, in all the drama of your arrival I completely forgot—something so important, I...'

She was tingling all over with secret excitement and happiness.

'Polly, darling.' He sounded huskily amused, holding her tenderly against him. 'Whatever it is, would you please tell me before I explode?'

She stifled a small laugh, wrapping her arms around him with a wriggle of pure joy. 'It's something that could mean I'll be putting on a bit of weight in the fairly near future...'

There was a stunned silence.

'You're pregnant!' His voice was thick with emotion.

Nodding dumbly, she felt an uncontrollable smile spreading over her face as she absorbed his powerful pleasure, the surge of male possessiveness and pride which seemed to ignite the intimacy between them.

'And you'd *forgotten*...?' He was half-teasing, half-disbelieving.

'Only temporarily,' she assured him, going hot with confusion. 'Believe me, I've thought of nothing else since I found out; it was just the...the turmoil of seeing you again...'

'I'm flattered—I think...'

'Oh, Marco...!'

'Darling. Are you all right? I mean, are you well? You've seen a doctor?'

'Yes, to all three. Everything is fine. I've never been fitter.'

'Have you told Ben yet?'

'No... I thought we could tell him the happy news together.'

'So you are happy to be having my baby?' he demanded softly.

'*Another* of your babies. Very. Can't you tell?'

'Tell that you're happy?' he murmured, his voice thick with passion, stroking his hand possessively down the length of her body, following each curve of breast, waist, hip and thigh with careful exploration. 'Or tell that you're pregnant?'

'Both...' Eyes shining, she drew him down to her. Every inch of her shivered with need.

Her feminine surrender aroused him with a sudden, powerful surge of desire. Capturing her mouth with his, and easing a place for himself between her legs, he claimed her hungrily and triumphantly, swallowing her soft gasps of pleasure, and Polly shut her eyes while body, mind and soul were transported to another dimension...

It was a long time afterwards when they stirred sufficiently to talk again. Then Marco scanned her hot face, and said slowly, 'This temporary amnesia of yours... If I hadn't come to England to find you, when were you going to tell me you were pregnant?'

She stared at him, then began to laugh softly.

'Darling, I didn't want to tell you over the phone. And...and I wanted to wait until you came back to me because you wanted to be with me, not because you knew I was having another baby. I...I think that's why it wasn't taking first place in my mind; I'd been hoping so desperately that you'd love me for myself, not because I was the mother of your children...'

His eyes darkened. *'Cara...'*

'You're my husband now,' she reminded him gently, touching his face with her hands, a fresh wave of tenderness coming over her as she saw the trace of anxiety in his eyes. 'You're Ben's father. The father of Ben's new little brother or sister. You don't seriously think I'd have done another disappearing trick?'

'Not seriously...no.' His eyes were intent on her face. 'But I can't forget those years, Polly.'

'I know. You can't forget—but you can forgive?'

'Yes,' he agreed quietly. 'Now that I understand, I can easily forgive. In fact, I think I am the luckiest man alive.' He cradled her against him and kissed her with a tender possessiveness more eloquent than words.

The family christening, at the farmhouse in Tuscany, was crowded with people generating a happy atmosphere. No hint of past feuds was allowed to dent the goodwill. Even Sophy was there, eye-catching in a scarlet sundress, 'between modelling assignments,' as she informed people, and surprising everyone by still being with Luciano, hanging on his arm with every sign of genuine affection.

Polly, in a short grey-blue silk dress which showed off her newly regained figure, her blonde hair worn long and simple the way Marco liked it best, stood in the family group for the photographer. In front of her, Ben proudly held his three-month old baby sister, a bundle of white in her christening robe.

Polly felt a happy glow as she thought about the last christening she'd attended, for Marietta's twins. Then she'd felt an outsider, wary of her welcome and weighed down with her guilty secret.

Today she felt at the heart of the family, of her own family and friends. Ruth and Tino were mingling and smiling, every inch the proud grandparents. Marco's two sisters were here, with their husbands, their children proving very satisfactory playmates for Ben, and Marietta's twins were just learning to walk, with Angela's little daughter Rosa holding them by the hands and leading them amongst the guests. Polly's father was here too, beaming delightedly at his newly acquired extended family, and Will, and Janie—who was Ben's godmother—and Giuliana and Mario, now firm friends of Polly's as well as Marco's.

Giuliana was the new baby's godmother. She'd just announced that she was expecting her own baby in seven months' time, a stroke of fortune she was insisting on attributing to Polly. 'You bring good luck, *cara*,' she told Polly as she stood nearby. 'The minute you asked me to be godmother, I became pregnant!'

'Possibly something Mario did had a bearing on the situation as well?' Marco suggested drily, his arm sliding round Polly's shoulders.

Amidst general laughter, Polly turned to smile at her husband, and he kissed her. It was a kiss of electrifying sensuality, the kind that excluded everyone else within a ten-foot radius.

'You look radiant,' he murmured huskily, when they finally broke apart.

'Do I?' she teased, pink-faced. 'I wonder why? Could it be having two adorable children and a husband to match?'

'Me? Adorable?' His grin melted her.

'You know it. Everyone adores you. You're a national hero, remember? *Il angelo custode*. I can't even suspect you of criminal connections any longer, can I?' she risked with a soft laugh. 'Not that I ever did! Truly!'

His eyes had darkened to ink-black, but he smiled wryly.

'I should think not. Sicily's guardian angel?'

'Mine, too.'

'Yours?'

'Think what could have happened if you hadn't been there that night in Cambridge?' she said, her eyes wide on his face.

The photographer was fussing about the composition of the group.

'Move in a little.' He was waving his hand. 'Ben, hold the baby a little higher...that's it, good boy...'

They bent to ensure that Ben, frowning with proud concentration, was holding his baby sister safely, and as they did so Rachel Angela Daretta stretched her fists in the air and woke up, staring quite happily, if rather unfocused, at her father, mother and brother in turn, revealing large grey-blue eyes in a heart-shaped face beneath a fluff of barley-blonde hair.

'She's quite pretty. Just like Mummy,' Ben announced. 'Only Mummy's got more teeth.'

'Smile for the camera, please...' the photographer demanded.

The shutter clicked just as Polly's and Marco's laughing eyes met; their love for each other was so incandescent it was to light up the pages of photo-albums for all the years to come...

EMILIE
RICHARDS

THE WAY
BACK HOME

As a teenager, Anna Fitzgerald fled an impossible
situation, only to discover that life on the streets was
worse. But she had survived. Now, as a woman,
she lived with the constant threat that the secrets of
her past would eventually destroy her new life.

1-55166-399-6
**AVAILABLE IN PAPERBACK
FROM SEPTEMBER, 1998**

CHRISTIANE HEGGAN

SUSPICION

Kate Logan's gut instincts told her that neither of her
clients was guilty of murder, and homicide detective
Mitch Calhoon wanted to help her prove it. What neither suspected was how dangerous the truth would be.

*"Christiane Heggan delivers a tale that will leave you
breathless."*

—Literary Times

1-55166-305-8
AVAILABLE IN PAPERBACK
FROM SEPTEMBER, 1998

4 FREE

books and a surprise gift!

We would like to take this opportunity to thank you for reading this Mills & Boon® book by offering you the chance to take FOUR more specially selected titles from the Presents™ series absolutely FREE! We're also making this offer to introduce you to the benefits of the Reader Service™—

- ★ FREE home delivery
- ★ FREE gifts and competitions
- ★ FREE monthly newsletter
- ★ Books available before they're in the shops
- ★ Exclusive Reader Service discounts

Accepting these FREE books and gift places you under no obligation to buy, you may cancel at any time, even after receiving your free shipment. Simply complete your details below and return the entire page to the address below. *You don't even need a stamp!*

YES! Please send me 4 free Presents books and a surprise gift. I understand that unless you hear from me, I will receive 6 superb new titles every month for just £2.30 each, postage and packing free. I am under no obligation to purchase any books and may cancel my subscription at any time. The free books and gift will be mine to keep in any case.

P8YE

Ms/Mrs/Miss/Mr ....Initials ....
BLOCK CAPITALS PLEASE

Surname ....

Address ....

....

....Postcode................................

Send this whole page to:
THE READER SERVICE, FREEPOST, CROYDON, CR9 3WZ
(Eire readers please send coupon to: P.O. BOX 4546, DUBLIN 24.)

MILLS & BOON®

Emma Darcy

The Collection

* * * *

This autumn Mills & Boon® brings you a powerful
collection of three full-length novels by an
outstanding romance author:

Always Love
To Tame a Wild Heart
The Seduction of Keira

Over 500 pages of love, seduction and intrigue.

Available from September 1998